DIAMONDS
to Die For

by DAVID W. RUDLIN

Copyright © 2012 David W. Rudlin
All rights reserved.

ISBN: 1482796589
ISBN-13: 9781482796582

*To my girls:
For every minute, of every day.*

ben tro·va·to [ben tr*uh*-vah-toh; *It.* ben traw-vah-taw]

---

adjective appropriate and characteristic even if untrue; happily invented or discovered.

FORWARD

One day you're lying on a couch in a crap college apartment drinking Popov vodka with your friend Dave, and you think you've got at least a little bit figured out – you're a junior - and you're laughing at your own dumb jokes and ripping ferociously into classmates who have been deliberately excluded from your little late-night fest, and Dave's laughing, too, and while the future seems scary you're certain that Dave's going to be in it, and that makes it a lot less troubling. The next thing you know, your hair's fallen out and you're buzzing what little is left down to the nub, and that expensive record player you had in that crap apartment has become as useless as a Pompeian wine cask, and other friends you thought would be there for the long haul have dropped dead from heart attacks and brain tumors and strange -*itis*-es you'd never heard of before but are suddenly quite common and surprise surprise the haul isn't long at all, and to top it off, you watch stupefied as Dave speaks fluent Japanese to his lovely wife, and this bizarre parlor trick he's picked up somewhere is incredible to you, so incredible, in fact, that you can't help but laugh inappropriately and uncontrollably until Dave looks at you with a what's-the-big-deal expression, and he's right, it's no big deal, he's been living in Tokyo for the last thirty years.

Then it turns out that the show-stopping fluent-Japanese sketch isn't the only topper. Here on your computer screen is Dave's first novel. *He's a writer?* You know Dave the student, and you've accepted Dave the ad man and even Dave the diamond dealer, as much of a stretch as that was, but now you're forced to deal with Dave the novelist whether you like it or not, and lucky for you the novel's terrifically good, because if it wasn't you'd have to lie to him, and you might not be able to do that successfully, since Dave has seen you drunk, stoned, flying on acid, humiliatingly sex-starved, and crying all over yourself, and knowing that he knows you longer and better than almost anybody else you just can't tell him it's great when it's not because he won't believe you.

But it *is* great. It would have blown me away even if I didn't know the guy who wrote it. I do, it did, and I'm really not all that surprised.

Ed Sikov
February 2013
New York City

CHAPTER 1

London, March 15, 8:30 AM

From the outside, #42 Farringdon Road doesn't look like much. Just down the road from London's Smithfield Meat Market, its soot-covered bricks are badly in need of cleaning. Several of its nine floors have no windows at all, and even the more fortunate get only tiny panes of thick, nearly opaque glass. It looks like the sort of place where accountants go to die.

Inside is a completely different story. For behind the deliberately unremarkable façade lie more than $8 billion worth of rough, unpolished diamonds, locked away in the basement vaults of the most powerful diamond company the world has ever known.

Delacroix.

Not surprisingly, Delacroix guards its fortune with the most advanced security system in Europe – if not the world. Walk through the bulletproof entrance doors, and they lock firmly behind you. Six feet ahead is a second, manned checkpoint which only staff and authorized visitors get past. Employees then swipe their photo IDs at a third set of locked doors while visitors must wait for a staff escort to take them upstairs.

Once inside the building, wandering the halls is physically impossible. Every 10 yards or so passage is blocked by electronic doors that can only be opened by swiping a personalized pass programmed to open some doors and not others – with access varying by rank, section, day and what's going on in the building. A marketing staff card won't open the door to the sales section, and a salesman can't invite himself into the legal department. Members of the executive committee can open all the hallway doors, but even they can't get inside the vaults. And only eight people are automatically admitted to the ultra-secure Client Area on the second floor.

As if that weren't enough to keep people where they're supposed to be, each swipe of a pass card shows up on a screen in the Security Office – so the guards know where everyone is every minute of the day.

Further security is provided by dozens of surveillance cameras. These feed into a basement-level Command Centre where teams of specialists stare at monitors, looking for the telltale signs of a tiny diamond being slipped into a French cuff or under a watchband.

In the 87 years #42 Farringdon Road has served as the sales and marketing headquarters of Delacroix, not a single diamond has ever gone missing. There have been no attempted robberies. Handbags sit openly on desks, as employees have complete – and justified – faith in the unseen system.

Which is why there was more disbelief than horror one brilliant summer morning when Maria Cortés, the weekday cleaning lady, tripped over a dead body lying in a pool of blood just inches away from the Client Area coffee machine.

CHAPTER 2

London, March 15, 8:33 AM

Maria screamed, looked up towards the ceiling, and fainted.

Before her head touched the carpet, an alarm went off. That was followed by the sound of heavy dead bolts dropping into the locked position. The green lights on the security pads next to each doorway switched to flashing red, preventing the doors from being opened by anyone without an Emergency Pass. Thick steel panels came thundering down to block all the windows. Armed guards – normally never seen in the tranquil corridors of #42 – went running down the halls to predetermined positions, eyes moving constantly, fingers twitching on the trigger guards of their AK-47's.

A voice accustomed to authority came over the loudspeaker. "Would everyone please stand up, put your hands on the desk nearest you, and remain in that position until you have been individually cleared by Security. I repeat: please stand with your hands in view, and remain standing until you have been cleared by Security. *This is not a drill.*"

Timothy Mathews, Head of Security, ran up the rear stairs to the second floor. He waved his Emergency Pass at the door, then swore loudly as the system triple-checked his credentials.

When he finally heard the lock click open, he barged through the door… and slipped on the blood-soaked carpet.

"A gentleman," was the first phrase that came to mind. Probably in his 60's, wearing an impeccably tailored Gieves & Hawkes suit with a pocket cravat and a tasteful Hermes tie. Longish silver hair, combed straight back and neatly trimmed. A large, heavy watch with an almost excessive amount of gold. Eyeglasses spilling out of the jacket pocket, the left lens slightly cracked. Skin that had clearly spent a lot of time in the sun and was then rewarded with generous helpings of expensive creams. Everything about him spoke of taste, sophistication and elegance. In fact, Mathews thought the gentleman would have looked quite peaceful, even happy – had it not been for the bullet hole in his chest and the shocking amount of blood.

The last time Matthews had seen a dead body had been during the Falklands business. In the nearly 30 years since, his focus had shifted from watching the horizon for troop movements, to searching a 17" screen for signs of nimble fingers trying to hide a diamond. He'd been trained to think like a thief and assume that what one *couldn't* see was precisely where a problem was most likely hiding. He had absolutely no idea how to deal with a homicide, nor any desire to do so.

"Call Scotland Yard!" he yelled at the nearby employees who were still standing frozen in position with their hands on their desks. "Dammit," Mathews shouted, "a man's been killed. You there, the lady with the glasses. Pick up the phone and call the police. Do it *now!*" The woman moved as if in a trance, but she made the call.

London, March 15, 8:33 AM

Matthews massaged his temples slowly, until the voice of his Second In Command coming through his earpiece called him back into the moment. "Tim, you're not going to believe this, but we've got nothing."

"What do you mean?"

"I mean there are no records of unauthorized entrances or exits last night. None of the night guards saw or heard anything unusual – much less a gunshot. We haven't had time to check all the surveillance tapes properly, but we fast-forwarded through the film from the camera over your head, and there is absolutely nothing. No people. No movement. Nothing."

"That can't be."

"I know. But it is."

Mathews stood up, and brushed off his clothes. God, what a mess. How was it possible that two men came in, one got killed, the other left – and the company's new $5.2 million security system didn't see a thing? That's exactly what the MD would ask him, just before reminding him the company reluctantly invested in the system only after Mathews swore it was both foolproof and mission-critical. The boss would be mad about the waste of money, embarrassed by the public failure, and terrified of what it meant for diamond security. People were going to get fired for this, and Matthews was certain his name would be at the top of the list.

Looking down at the corpse lying peacefully on the floor, Mathews felt a tinge of envy.

CHAPTER 3

London, March 15, 9:30 AM

Chief Inspector Ian McLean had been on the Metropolitan Police force for 23 years. During that time he'd racked up a better-than-average conviction rate, but even he saw himself as more Lieutenant Colombo than Inspector Poirot. He wasn't unusually bright. He could count the number of sudden insights he'd had on the fingers of one hand. He worked hard, but not obsessively. His greatest strength, as one of his early performance reviews put it, was "he keeps plodding on until the job gets done".

Yet somewhat to his own surprise, McLean rarely exploded under pressure. That made him an asset in politically charged or other sensitive cases. But what many of his superiors didn't know was the price of his equilibrium was a tendency to be cynical and sarcastic with the people below him, particularly when things weren't going well.

As promised to be the case with the body that lay at his feet.

No visible scratches or other signs of a struggle. Forensics would have to do a more careful check of the scrapings, but McLean could see nothing under the fingernails. No bumps or bruises. The man's shirt was still neatly tucked into his trousers. In fact, nothing looked out of the ordinary at all, except for the bullet hole in the chest and the pool of blood around the body.

By this point the security systems inside the building had been turned off, and the "stay right where you are" order rescinded. A large crowd of employees had gathered at a respectful distance from the crime scene, eager to see what was going on. McLean hated lookie-loos with a passion, though he supposed it was only human to stare at another's tragedy while counting oneself lucky – the *better him than me* joy that lurked just beneath the pasted-on looks of concern. "Anyone know who this is?" he asked the crowd. No response. "Perhaps you've seen him before, but don't know his name? Those of you in the back, please move forward so you can get a better look. Some of you may not have seen a dead body before, and I'll grant it's not pleasant. But speed is critically important to catching whoever did this, and that makes it essential we discover the identify of the victim as soon as possible. So please, if you can, come over here and see if you recognize him."

One by one the staff marched past, looking at first in fascination, then quickly turning away in horror. They *thought* they'd be interested; they were shocked at their own naiveté. While there was surprisingly little gore – McLean made a mental note – there was quite a lot of blood soaking into the carpet around the victim's head and shoulders. That, plus the pale green color of the victim's face as the body began the first stages of rigor mortis, made the scene tough to look

London, March 15, 9:30 AM

at for the uninitiated. And it was all for naught; not a single person could recall having seen the victim before.

It was still too early to call the man a "murder victim". Suicide was a possibility – he'd have to wait for the coroner's report to see whether there were any powder burns on the victim's hands – but McLean thought this unlikely. After all, if the man had shot himself, where was the gun? And why break *into* the most secure building in Europe just to end one's life? Jumping *out* a window would have been much easier. Or if you had your heart set on firearms, why not shoot yourself in the comfort of your own home?

Perhaps the victim managed to break in, and was shot by a frightened employee? Possible, but if so the killer was almost certain to be a security guard; no one else would be permitted to have a gun. And if shots were fired in the line of duty, why not just step forward and acknowledge what happened? It was far too early to jump to any conclusions, but for now the smart money was on murder.

McLean stood as the forensic team entered the area and began to dust for fingerprints. They're going to have fun, he thought. In the initial briefing he got on the ride over from Scotland Yard, McLean learned that #42 Farringdon Road has more than 1,200 employees and up to 100 overseas staff and visitors arriving each week. It would take ages to track all those people down, get them printed, and check those against the prints Forensics was now lifting. If they got lucky there would be one or more sets of prints that couldn't be matched to someone with a legitimate reason for being in the building. If so, they'd start checking the files for matches with known criminals. If all went smoothly McLean might have a lead in, say, just under two months. Half-amused by that thought, he walked over to the vending machine, asked a tech whether it had been dusted for prints, and when he got an answer in the affirmative pressed the button for an espresso; something told him his brain was going to need all the help it could get today.

As he watched the investigators examine the body, McLean's eye was drawn to the victim's left wrist. He was still wearing a diamond-studded Piaget watch that must have cost at least $50,000. If this had been a robbery it was a bad one; either that or the perpetrator had been frightened off before the job could be finished. So far no one had found the electronic ID card the victim would have needed to enter the building and move around; perhaps the killer took it. But more significantly they hadn't found a single clue as to the identity of the victim. No wallet. No hotel cards or house keys. No name tags or monograms on his clothes. But McLean didn't have to work too hard to come up with explanations for all of this. Most men stop putting their names on their clothing at about age seven. If the victim was married and his wife was at home, he might have gone out without his keys and counted on her to let him back in. Less likely to leave without his wallet, but perhaps that was stolen together with the ID card. So maybe it all meant nothing.

Or maybe the killer had deliberately taken everything that might identify the victim – and only those things. That would explain leaving the watch behind. But why would anyone go to the trouble of hiding someone's identity, and then leave the body in full view of everyone who came into a very crowded office – an office teeming with surveillance cameras?

McLean felt the early rumblings of a tension headache. Whoever did this had ice in his veins, and balls the size of cantaloupes in his pants. What's more, he wanted people to admire his handiwork. The last thing McLean needed right now was a criminal mastermind who got his jollies from demonstrating how much smarter he was than the police. That was catnip to Britain's tabloids, which meant the police commissioner would be even more unrealistic than usual in his demands for a rapid arrest.

Just then a junior forensic technician called out "Found a piece of paper in the coin pocket!"

"Don't just stand there looking proud of yourself, man, what does it say?"

The technician unfolded the piece of paper and saw angry black letters nearly an inch high. "It says, REMEMBER GABORONE. What the hell is Gaborone, guv?"

That, thought McLean, is an excellent question.

CHAPTER 4

London, March 15, 2:00 PM

McLean clasped his hands behind his head, leaned backwards, and tried to crack his aching spine over the top of the chair. At nearly 6'3" he had to scrunch up in order to see the undersized screens on Scotland Yard's antique computers. Add a stubborn insistence that 45 was too young for a man to wear reading glasses, and desk research was about as pleasurable for McLean as a trip to the dentist.

Still, it had to be done. And while he could order one of his subordinates to look for something specific, at this stage even McLean didn't know what he was after. So he decided to cast his net as widely as possible, and Googled "diamonds". Less than a second later he had nearly 31 million results, the very first of which was "Delacroix". "You'll get your chance to speak" McLean said out loud, "but wait your turn. We'll start with a more impartial source, I think."

McLean clicked on an industry website, skimmed the section on how diamonds were formed, then slowed down when he got to History:

The first diamonds were discovered in Golconda, India about 4,000 years ago. They were few and far between, and their scarcity meant that for centuries diamonds were available only to kings and queens, moguls and maharajas. But all that changed one afternoon in 1866 when a small boy playing beside the banks of the Orange River in what is now South Africa discovered a large and shiny pebble. He gave it to a neighbor who collected unusual stones – and who realized it was, in fact, a brownish yellow diamond. The stone was cut, polished, and named "Eureka". At 21.25 carats it was reasonably large, but otherwise unimpressive. Yet no other diamond has had nearly the same impact on both southern Africa and the world.

News of the find spread rapidly, and when in 1871 a second diamond was found on a hill in the town of Kimberley, thousands of men descended on the site, bearing shovels and dreams. Their combined ant-like efforts created what became known as "The Big Hole". With rudimentary skills and only a passing interest in safety, these men gambled their lives in hopes of finding a fortune below ground. Few did.

One of those who succeeded was Thomas Weil, the founder of Delacroix.

As he read on, McLean learned the secret to Weil's success was not greater persistence, superior mining techniques or even a lucky find. It was the realization that as long as sellers of rough diamonds greatly outnumbered buyers, it would be nearly impossible to make a decent profit. So he set about buying up the claims of his erstwhile competitors, using cash generated from providing mundane services like pumping water out of the mines. After a few downturns – inevitable in a cyclical business like diamonds – Weil controlled enough of Kimberley that he was able to dictate prices to the buyers.

Precisely as Delacroix does today, McLean thought.

Weil's second brainstorm was possibly even more transformational than the first. Traditionally buyers had cherry-picked the diamonds they wanted – usually the larger, better quality stones – leaving the miners with piles of lesser goods that were effectively worthless. So Weil packaged the good with the bad, and informed customers they must either buy the whole thing or nothing at all. By that point he controlled so much of the diamond market the buyers had no choice but to accept his terms. As a result Weil was able to sell far more of his production than anyone ever had, making him a very rich man and dramatically increasing the number of diamonds available to the world. For the first time in history diamonds were accessible not only to the aristocracy, but also to the reasonably well-off masses. India may have given us the first diamonds, but South Africa gave us the most. That is why, to this day, most people think diamonds all come from South Africa.

McLean had to admit he was one of those people. But as he scrolled down the chart listing the diamond producing nations by value, he saw that South Africa came in fourth, behind Russia, Canada, Angola and – the biggest of them all – Botswana.

Botswana? McLean's mind flashed back to that insufferable novel about the #1 Women's Detective Agency – or whatever – that Edith had tried to force him to read. Every night he would dutifully open the book, pretend to read until he saw a look of satisfaction on his wife's face, and then shut the damn thing and fall instantly asleep. The next night he would repeat the process, having first jumped ahead 20-25 pages to reflect his "progress".

From an earlier case linked – just barely – to Cambodia, McLean knew that the CIA website was the place to go for country information. So he typed "Botswana + CIA" into Google. The result told him that when Botswana gained its independence from Britain in 1967, it was one of the poorest countries on the planet. It had less than 4 kilometers of paved roads, not enough to reach from the airport to the center of town. Much of the country was illiterate. But in 1968 diamonds were discovered, and almost overnight the country's transformation began. By 2004 Botswana was what the UN calls a "middle income country", ranked as the most open economy and best credit risk in all of Africa. Diamonds brought the people – called Batswana -- from bushmen to businessmen in less than a generation.

Today diamonds account for 1/3 of Botswana's GDP, 50% of government revenue, and over 75% of export income. One in four Batswana is employed by the diamond industry, either directly or indirectly. And as the source of more than 26% of the world's diamonds by value, it is arguably the most powerful player in the $70 billion global diamond industry.

Its capital is Gaborone.

"Well how about that," McLean said as he once again cracked his back over the top of his chair. "An actual, honest-to-goodness clue."

CHAPTER 5

London, March 16, 10:30 AM

Darren Franklin had been the head of Scotland Yard for nearly 11 years. He was probably the last of the Old School Coppers, the men who thought policing was about knowing the community, maintaining a broad network of confidential informants, and being able to spot a liar from 20 paces. He wasn't particularly comfortable with the so-called "new policing", which seemed to involve inordinate amounts of time sitting in front of a computer screen and practically none walking the streets. Franklin knew he was powerless to stop the change, but in the two years remaining before his mandatory retirement things were going to be done his way. Every time.

Recently that stubbornness had found a home not only in his behavior but also squarely upon his face. McLean was not looking forward to the discussion he was about to have.

"Sir, I need your approval to go to Gaborone."

"And what, pray tell, is Gaborone?"

"Not what, sir. Where. It's the capital of Botswana."

"You do realize you're not moving the ball forward, don't you McLean?"

So the Inspector laid the whole thing out for his skeptical boss. The body that shouldn't have been there. The failure of a state-of-the-art security system. The near-total absence of clues. And the one thin thread he had to pull on: the note saying REMEMBER GABORONE. Little by little Franklin's expression changed, and by the time McLean was done with his tale the irritation on Franklin's face had been replaced by complete bafflement.

"So faced with a mystery worthy of Agatha Christie, you're telling me the single most important thing you can do right now is leave the scene of the crime and all the actual *evidence*, and go wandering around Gee, Ga... whatever the hell it is in hopes of stumbling across the meaning of a two-word note."

McLean took a deep breath, hoping to keep the rising irritation out of his voice. "It isn't just the note, sir. Gaborone is where all the lines converge. It's the capital of Botswana, which is the world's largest producer of diamonds, and Delacroix is the biggest employer in the country."

"And what does all that have to do with the price of tea in China?"

"At this point I'm not sure, Chief. But I'm not going to find out by sitting here looking at the Internet. I need to get out there and start asking questions."

For the first time since the discussion began, Franklin's face relaxed – just a bit. "Planning to do some actual investigating, are we?"

McLean knew there was a time and place for shameless toadying, and that was right here, right now. "It's the only way to crack a case, sir."

The Chief leaned back in his chair, and dropped his arms onto the armrests. The body language was promising. "Suppose I agree to this little safari of yours. Who's going to look after things at this end?"

"I was thinking Thomas could call me with a daily progress report, and I could issue marching orders through him."

Franklin smiled triumphantly. "Thomas, eh? Is it possible you're finally coming to realize the boy has his uses after all?"

McLean reddened. "I'd say the jury is still out on that, sir. But after three years he should be able to handle something as straightforward as a progress report."

"Especially considering how much time and effort you personally invested in training him."

McLean was tempted to respond with chapter and verse. In his estimation Thomas remained one of the least capable cadets he had ever encountered. The boy meant well, but he was thick. Lacked common sense. Would forget to exhale if you didn't remind him. But for some reason Chief Franklin had a soft spot for the young man, and nothing McLean could say was going to change that.

"This will be good for him, sir. It's a chance to show us he can manage without direct supervision. Maybe it's just the opportunity he needs."

The Chief chuckled. "You always were a lousy liar, though full marks for trying."

"Sir, I know budgets are tight, and with my bad back the thought of spending 10 hours on an airplane is hardly exciting. If I could, I'd just call the Gaborone Police Department and do the whole thing over the phone."

"So why don't you?"

"What would I say to them? 'I've got a dead guy with a two-line note in his pocket. Can you help?' They'd think it was a prank phone call."

"One could hardly blame them for that." Franklin let his head drop onto the back of his chair. "So this on-the-ground investigation you're planning to conduct: where will you start?"

"Probably with Delacroix. The body was found in their head office; if anyone knows what REMEMBER GABORONE means, it's them."

Franklin sat up straight in his armchair, joined his hands together, and held them over his mouth. For several minutes he was silent, but McLean could practically hear his boss's mind racing. Finally he placed his palms on the table and looked McLean in the eye. "Be very careful, son. Delacroix has friends in very high places. There is only one private citizen in the entire country with the right to land a helicopter in central London. That man is Clarence Weil, chairman of the company. Got personal permission from Her Most Royal Majesty. And when our beloved Queen goes to Ascot each year, she sits in the Delacroix box while Weil whispers sweet nothings in her ear. So if I get a call from on high, asking me why my men are bothering that nice Mr. Weil, I'll have your guts for garters."

"I'll be careful, sir. And my investigation will be at a level far, far below the level of 'that nice Mr. Weil'."

Franklin gave the tiniest nod of his head, and gestured for the Travel Approval form, which he promptly signed. McLean was about to make his first-ever trip to The Dark Continent. As he walked out the door he heard Franklin call after him: "You never did tell me, where the hell is Botswhatsit?"

"Southern Africa, sir." McLean liked the way that sounded coming out of his mouth, and decided right then and there he'd try to work it into his conversation as much as possible over the next few days. But his excitement disappeared as soon as he went online to book his flights. Gaborone is one of those places "you can't get to from here", unless Here happens to be South Africa, Zimbabwe or Zambia. Botswana has its own airline – Botswana Air – but it only flies as far as its nearest neighbors. The just-about-tolerable flight to Africa would only be the beginning of McLean's journey; if he took the cheapest available option in accordance with government policy, he'd be lucky to reach his hotel within 24 hours of leaving London. The thought of spending most of that time trapped in an Economy Class seat made McLean wish he'd been a little less dismissive of teleconferencing.

That feeling intensified when he made a quick stop at his small red brick home in Chiswick in order to pack his bags.

"You're going *where*?" his wife Edith asked, her Scottish brogue untouched by 25 years of life in London.

"Southern Africa. Botswana, to be exact."

"Why in God's name would you do that?"

"It's work."

"Silly me. All this time I thought you worked in London, not Africa."

McLean counted to five, silently. "Edith, the crime was committed in London, but the trail leads to a country called Botswana, in southern Africa."

"And you have to go yourself, even with your bad back? Why can't Thomas go? Isn't it time he got pushed out of the nest?

"Sweetheart, thank you for worrying about my increasingly decrepit body. But the case involves Delacroix…"

"The diamond people?"

"That's them. And they are very well connected, so someone with a bit more experience and finesse than Thomas can muster is required."

"Wait – wasn't there something about this in the morning paper? There was a shooting, but no one saw it, and no one knows who the dead guy is?"

"A little off on the details, but yes, that's the one."

"Why didn't you tell me you were working on a diamond case? That's very exciting!"

"Well, I won't be working on it – or anything at all – if I miss my flight. Can you help me throw some things together?"

Edith smiled indulgently. "That, my dear, is your problem. One does not throw things into a suitcase; one carefully packs them. That way you won't be more wrinkly than Yoda when you're meant to be representing queen and country overseas."

"I fear you may be confusing me with James Bond."

"Little chance of that, dear" Edith said playfully as she pushed her husband away from the suitcase and began re-folding his clothes.

CHAPTER 6

Antwerp, December 17, 2:00 PM

Daniel Stern was troubled. On the table in front of him sat the largest rough diamond he had ever seen. At 138 carats it was also one of the largest diamonds to be offered for sale in the last few years. And it wasn't just big. From what Daniel could tell – which he had to admit wasn't much, given the stone's heft and the thick layer of "frost" on the surface – it was reasonably clean of the internal imperfections called "piques" that lower a diamond's value. If he was right, he should end up with a polished diamond of 30-40 carats. With a decent color and quality – say H/VS1 – that would bring $65,000 - 70,000 *per carat*. Quickly doing the calculations in his head, Daniel realized he was looking at a price tag of between $1.9 and $4 million.

The size of those numbers sent Daniel's imagination into high gear. What if the finished stone turned out to be D-Flawless? Sure, the odds were against it: just 0.001% of diamonds mined are both colorless and free of imperfections when polished. But if a miracle happened, the price tag would be closer to $8 million. Never before had Daniel been offered anything remotely as valuable.

And that was precisely the problem.

Daniel made a decent living cutting and polishing rough diamonds of one-to-three carats. He had a reputation for good quality, well-proportioned diamonds. He had a reasonable list of leading jewelers and private customers he supplied. But the biggest stone he'd ever cut was just over four carats, and that was more than a decade ago. He was certainly *not* one of the people who got a call when a Special – a diamond larger than 10.8 carats – was discovered. Daniel Stern had limits, and everyone in the trade knew it.

There are only a handful of men in the entire world with the skill, experience and courage needed to cut a massive rough diamond like the one on the table before him. While the procedures are the same as for smaller stones, the greater size multiplies both the complexity and the risk exponentially. There are hundreds of different ways to cut a 138-carat diamond, starting with a single stone that tries to preserve as much of the original shape as possible, and ending with dozens of round, square, oval, tear-drop and cushion-shaped stones, each in the size, color and quality most likely to sell in the current marketplace. A *diamantaire* had to have both the vision to imagine what was possible and the hard-nosed financial acumen to calculate which option would yield the greatest profit.

The diamond also has a say in the matter. While diamonds are the hardest material known to man, they are not invulnerable. In fact, if tapped along the grain a diamond will cleave like butter being cut with a warm knife. Hit a weak spot, and the diamond can shatter – leaving the cutter with nothing but extremely expensive diamond powder good only for coating drill bits and polishing wheels. So before a cutter picks up his tools, he gets to know the stone better than he knows his wife or lover. With large diamonds he – it's almost always a he – may spend up to a year doing nothing all day but looking deep into the heart of the diamond. With a frosted stone like the one Daniel was now holding, after several weeks or months of staring the *diamantaire* would cut a "window" – a slice off the side of the stone that makes it easier to see inside – and start the process all over again.

Daniel knew all this, but he'd never *done* it. So why, he asked himself, is this man I've never seen before offering this amazing diamond *to me*? Maybe there's something wrong inside the stone he thinks I'm too inexperienced to see. Or that I'll make a ridiculously high offer, just for the chance to play with the big boys. Well, there's one way to find out.

"How much do you want for it?" Daniel asked, while doing his best to look fairly bored by the whole thing.

"Whatever you think is fair."

What had started as a gentle tingling of alarm bells was now a deafening roar. Competition for a diamond this large and this beautiful is cutthroat. For every diamantaire given a chance to bid, there are 20 more who don't get their calls returned. The Chosen are then given as little as 20 minutes to inspect the stone before submitting a bid that can easily run into the tens of millions of dollars. Sellers play buyers off against each other, leaking bids (real or otherwise) in order to drive up the price. Private viewings and "whatever you think is fair" have no place in the world of Specials.

Unless the diamond had been stolen. Or smuggled out of its country of origin. Or came from one of the countries not approved by the Kimberley Process, meaning it could be a blood diamond -- diamonds mined in a war zone and sold to finance the overthrow of a legitimate government. Trading in blood diamonds did happen, but only among men who consider Russian Roulette an interesting diversion. And Daniel was terrified of guns.

The smart thing to do would be to make a low bid, let it be rejected, and leave with nothing more than a story worth telling the guys over beers Friday night at the Kulminator bar on Vleminckveld:

"What's new, Laurens?"

"Nothing."

"Anything interesting happen to you, Pieter?"

"Nope."

"And you, Daniel?"

"A complete stranger offered me a 138-carater for whatever price I felt was fair. But I could tell it was a blood diamond so I told him to leave my office before I called the police."

On the other hand...

Daniel knew this was his one chance to rise above the million or so men, women and children who cut diamonds for a living, and join the ranks of the elite cutters whose names are known everywhere from 47th Street in New York, to Opera House in Mumbai, to Ginza in Tokyo. This stone was a chance to transform his life, both professionally and financially. Instead of being yet another small businessman on the fringes of the diamond industry, overnight he would become a player. All the people who had looked down on him – especially his arrogant idiot of a banker – would have to change their tune. And instead of telling stories about the great diamond he almost bought, he could tell them about the fantastic, one of a kind diamond he actually cut.

His father had always told him: great fortune doesn't come without great risk. Well, Papa, this one's for you.

Daniel swallowed hard, and looked up into the deep blue eyes of the man who had chosen Daniel apparently at random. Without having a clue as to how he was going to pay for it, Daniel said with a nonchalance that surprised him, "$1.5 million".

"Deal", the man said, and got up to leave.

"Deal", said Daniel, but the man was already out the door.

CHAPTER 7

Johannesburg, May 17, 8:30 a.m.

McLean arrived in Johannesburg after spending a sleepless night on the 11-hour flight from London Heathrow. It had been every bit as uncomfortable and unpleasant as he'd expected, and the huge line at Passport Control wasn't helping his mood one bit. After 30 minutes of finding himself getting further and further away – everyone in front of him seemed to be holding a place for an extended family that magically expanded the closer they got to the counter – he decided to pull rank. He found a South African inspector, flashed his badge, and asked to go through the line for officials. The inspector maintained his bored but threatening expression, said nothing, and pointed him back to the line.

It took nearly an hour to clear Immigration, and a further 20 minutes to get his bag. McLean wanted nothing more than a proper breakfast before transferring to Air Botswana for the final leg of his journey. Those hopes were quickly dashed. There was no shortage of shops selling Dashiki shirts and African masks made in China and "official merchandise" from the 2010 World Cup a year before, but there wasn't a single place in the departure terminal to have even a stale bun. He grumpily tried to satisfy his stomach with a cup of Rooibus tea at one of the pay-as-you-go departure lounges, but his mouth refused to cooperate after the third sip of the smelly herbal brew. Did these people learn *nothing* under colonialism?

It was after 1 PM when he arrived at Sir Seretse Khama International Airport in Botswana. As he walked down the stairs from the Air Botswana prop plane, the heat hit him like a slap in the face – with the slap delivered by Mohammad Ali. The sun was oppressively hot, but it was like a cool breeze compared to the heat that seemed to explode off the tarmac. As he entered the small terminal building, he saw the staff doing the only sensible thing in the current conditions: napping. After nearly 10 minutes, a truck hauling the luggage from the plane pulled up, and the driver got out. No one inside the terminal stirred. It was only when one of the passengers – a portly gentlemen whose nose showed all the signs of regular, excessive alcohol intake – went the wrong way through the entrance in an effort to reclaim his bag that anyone moved. Eventually all the luggage was passed by hand through a hole in the terminal wall, and placed at random on the floor. It was up to the passengers to take over from there.

Despite much shorter lines, Passport Control at Gaborone wasn't much faster than it had been in Johannesburg. More than 30 minutes after touchdown McLean was finally through, and he went to the small Currency Exchange to change some pounds sterling into the local currency – *pula*, which according to the leaflet that came with his receipt, is a Tswana word meaning "rain". The Inspector decided that this name was eminently sensible; after all, in an agrarian

Johannesburg, May 17, 8:30 a.m.

economy in a land where droughts are commonplace, rain is money for the local population. Feeling enlightened and proud of his own cleverness in equal measure, McLean strode briskly out the door – expecting to be met by a representative of the Botswana police. His confidence quickly flagged when he discovered there wasn't another human in sight, all of the other passengers having been picked up while McLean was changing money. He did a walk-around, just in case there were multiple entrances and he was at the wrong one. All he found were sun, heat, and flies. Surveying the broad, empty vista before him while wiping sweat off the back of his neck, McLean grew pensive. "It's a wonder they bother to get up in the morning," he muttered to himself.

Eventually a 20-year-old white Toyota pulled up, and slowed to a stop. The driver got out, scratched himself, smiled, and said "Taxi?" Not knowing when he'd get a second offer, Inspector McLean buried his misgivings and asked to be taken to Gaborone's only 4-star establishment, The Grand Palm Hotel Casino Resort. It had taken quite a bit of effort to get the bean counters in London to sign off on lodging with the word "casino" in the name. But after he'd forced them to look at expedia.com, and showed them a search for Gaborone hotels generated just six names – four of which were fully booked – they reluctantly agreed. McLean was looking forward to seeing what Las Vegas looked like with an African accent.

As the old Toyota bumped and sputtered along the surprisingly broad highway, McLean pulled out his Blackberry. No signal. While that might prove to be a problem later on, for now he was quite content to have an excuse for looking out the window at the scenery. He had to admit what he was seeing was not at all what he'd expected. There was the red dirt and stunted trees shown in movies like Meryl Streep's *Out Of Africa*. And occasionally he caught a glimpse of an outdoor market or a woman in a blindingly colorful caftan carrying a huge basket on her head. But for the most part it reminded him of the trip to Australia he and his wife had taken for their 10th anniversary. It wasn't nearly as developed as, say, Sydney, but it was right up there with some of the suburban towns they'd seen on the drive to the Hunter Valley. There were shiny glass buildings, a Lexus dealer, and a surprising number of banks. Ads for mobile phones were everywhere – even more insistent than what he was used to ignoring in London. With each additional sign of civilization, McLean felt himself relax a little. He hadn't realized that he had been worried about coming to Africa until those worries started to fade away.

30 minutes after leaving the airport, the taxi deposited McLean at the entrance to the hotel – where the bellman showed no interest in helping with his bags. Never one to stand on ceremony, McLean pulled out the handle on his battered Samsonite and headed for Reception under his own power. The staff at the front desk found his reservation quickly, but when he asked if there were any messages for him from the police they suddenly discovered they had other important matters to attend to. After glancing briefly at the tiny gift shop's motley assortment of mosquito spray, sun block and elephant-themed neckties, he went to his room.

Johannesburg, May 17, 8:30 a.m.

McLean hadn't been expecting the high rollers' suite at Caesar's Palace, but was still disappointed in the standard room at what was supposed to be the best hotel in the country. It was of a reasonable size... for London. But compared with the vast expanse of Africa he could see out the window, it was stingy at best. The fittings were at least 20 years old, and tatty. Bed. Desk. One lounge chair. TV. And that was about it. It looked like any room at any worn-out Holiday Inn anywhere in the world. The only thing faintly African was the bottle of mosquito repellent on the desk, and a note from hotel management strongly urging guests to "apply liberally" given the threat of malaria. "Ah, malaria!" McLean said out loud. "Just the thing to take home as a souvenir of my stay at this luxurious hotel."

Once his two-minute familiarization tour was over, McLean hung his clothes in the closet, dialed "0" and asked the operator to connect him with the Gaborone Police Service. A woman with a melodic and quite proper English accent answered the phone immediately, which reminded McLean that Botswana had been a British protectorate from 1910 until 1966, and that English was one of two official languages (Setswana being the other). Patting himself on the back for doing his homework before packing his bags, McLean began his approach.

"This is Inspector McLean of the Metropolitan Police Department in London. I arrived about an hour ago, and was expecting to meet your Detective Motswagae or his representative at the airport. If he was there I couldn't find him, and made my way to the hotel on my own."

Silence.

"I'm hoping he's there with you."

"Inspector, Detective Motswagae is indeed here, but he is tied up with an important guest from London who arrived just this afternoon."

McLean knew he was tired, and therefore likely to turn snappy. He forced himself to take a deep, cleansing breath in service of cross-border understanding and harmony. "I think there may have been a slight mix-up. *I* am the visitor from London Detective Motswagae was supposed to meet, and as you can tell from the fact I'm calling regarding his whereabouts, I am not with him."

"Did you say you were from the police?"

"Yes, I did. The London Metropolitan Police. Scotland Yard. In London. And I'm expected. So would it be possible to get the Detective for me, please?"

"I will have him call you as soon as he finishes his meeting with the gentleman from overseas."

McLean dug his fingernails into the palms of his hands. "Apparently I am not making myself clear. *I* am the gentlemen from overseas who is scheduled to meet with Detective Motswagae. Could you bring him to the phone for me, please?"

"I'm sorry, but he is meeting with the representative from Delacroix who arrived this morning, and has asked not to be disturbed."

Johannesburg, May 17, 8:30 a.m.

Inspector McLean was momentarily speechless. This was strange indeed. Delacroix wouldn't interfere with a police investigation into a murder that took place in *their* head office. Would they?

Perhaps they'd sent someone down here to clear the way for him, maybe even the portly gentlemen who tried to get his own bags at the airport. Reminding himself that the people of Botswana dislike public confrontations of any kind, McLean decided to give diplomacy one last try. "Of course, ma'am, we're working very closely with Delacroix on this issue. However I'm not sure who they sent down here; was it, by any chance, a man in his mid-50's, rather round, white hair and a – forgive me – bulbous nose?"

"I'm not sure I should be giving out this information, but no, that description doesn't match the gentleman at all."

"I suspect there's been a breakdown in communications somewhere. I was on the 1 o'clock flight from Johannesburg, and the man I described was the only other European on the flight."

"I believe it is customary for executives of Delacroix to travel by company plane."

Puzzled and faintly irritated, Inspector McLean hung up without saying another word.

CHAPTER 8

Gaborone, March 17, 4:20 p.m.

Pulling the red and brown cover off the bed and kicking off his shoes, McLean lay down for a quick nap. The combination of jet lag and the African heat was making him feel like he'd gone 10 rounds with Mike Tyson, and the two beers he'd rescued from his room's mini-fridge weren't helping. He'd barely closed his eyes when the phone rang. And rang. And rang. Either people in this country are extraordinarily patient, he thought, or whoever is calling knows I'm in the room and won't take silence for an answer.

His annoyance quickly disappeared when he finally answered the phone and the caller identified herself as an assistant to Detective Motswagae. "Mr. Motswagae is available to see you now." McLean resisted the urge to make a snide remark about Mr. Motswagae's sense of his own importance, and limited his response to "That's excellent. How do I get there?"

"There is a police car waiting for you at the hotel entrance."

The Inspector thanked her and rung off, wondering whether the schizophrenic reception he was getting was intended to put him in his place in advance of the discussions ahead or was simply the result of incompetence. He splashed some room-temperature water – the best the spigot marked "cold" could muster – on his face in the hope of waking up his aching brain, put his tie and shoes back on, and headed out the door to the waiting squad car. The journey took him down Nelson Mandela Drive, which seemed to be the broadest street in town. Then up Independence Avenue to Botswana Street; the nation was clearly proud of its recent history and development

Less than 15 minutes later he found himself seated in a small room painted in what once was probably white but that was now decorated with smoke stains, sweat marks, and dead bugs. A ceiling fan turned lazily, more successful at moving the hot air around than actually cooling it off. McLean was sweating everywhere from the top of his increasingly bald head to the underside of his little toe; the more common places sweat accumulates were drenched and of considerable embarrassment to the usually fastidious inspector. The heat had encouraged his jet lag to mount another attack, and the mosquito spray he'd covered himself in as his only precaution against malaria smelled so sickly sweet it made him gag if he breathed through his nose. Nonetheless he dug deep into his reserves of artificial respect, wondered why the well-dressed detective sitting across the table didn't appear to be sweating at all, and began.

"Detective, thank you for seeing me on such short notice. The Metropolitan Police Department is greatly in your debt. I know you have a very busy schedule, so with your permission I will – as they say – cut to the chase."

He waited for a reaction.

Gaborone, March 17, 4:20 p.m.

"It's a Hollywood expression."

Still nothing.

"I'm here investigating a murder that took place in London three days ago."

"I see," said Motswagae mildly.

McLean waited for more, but after an uncomfortable 30 seconds of silence the Inspector again took the lead.

"The body was found in a most unusual place. In an office building, and a very secure one at that."

Again McLean waited for a response that did not come.

"It was at Delacroix, you see. The diamond company. Their headquarters at #42 Farringdon Road in London. Extremely well protected, as you'd expect – given the value of the diamonds on the premises. State of the art security system. Electronic doors every 10 yards. Hundreds of security cameras. You can't move a muscle in that building without someone seeing you."

At last Detective Motswagae spoke. "So then you'll have the murder – and the murderer – captured on tape."

"Ah, well, there's the sticky wicket."

"I'm not sure I follow."

"Both the main security system and the fail-safe showed absolutely nothing abnormal during the period in which the murder was committed. No one unusual came in. No one unusual went out. It's a crime that left no trace."

"Other than the corpse."

"Other than the corpse," McLean agreed.

"Was there a failure of the security system? Perhaps it was switched off? A power failure, maybe?"

"No, nothing like that. We checked."

Motswagae looked up towards the lazy ceiling fan, the traces of a smile around the corners of his mouth revealing dazzlingly white teeth. "Was the victim a Batswana?"

"No sir. He appears to be European, white, male, maybe 60 years old."

"I see." And for an uncomfortably long time, that's all Detective Motswagae did. Finally: "Inspector, this is indeed a fascinating case. But while I am honored to be paid a visit by a senior official from Her Majesty's Police, I am struggling to understand why you felt it necessary to fly all the way to Botswana to discuss a murder that took place in *your* country, involving a citizen not of Botswana but of, again, *your* country."

At last McLean found himself on familiar ground. Motswagae was observing the First Commandment of police work: don't let someone else's tough cases get dumped on you. But this one was one game McLean played at an all-pro level. "Two reasons, sir. First, the Delacroix connection. I'm told they're the largest company in Botswana, and employ – directly or indirectly – about 20% of the population."

"That hardly seems grounds for suspecting our involvement."

"No one is implying anything of the sort. That brings me to the main reason I'm here: a clue."

"And what might that be, Inspector?"

"A piece of paper with the words REMEMBER GABORONE written in capital letters."

Detective Motswagae was quiet for several minutes. Finally he exhaled heavily, and said – expressively – "Hmm".

"Does that phrase have any meaning to you? Is it a slogan used here, perhaps during a time of war or revolution?"

"Botswana has never known war, Inspector. We are a peaceful people who like to settle our differences through amiable discussion. I hope you will stay in Botswana long enough to see for yourself that not all African nations fit the Western stereotype."

McLean and his stomach were becoming exasperated; his face remained implacable. "Detective, you and I are both policemen. As much as any human can, we approach the world with no preconceptions, and let the evidence speak for itself."

For the first time, Motswagae smiled. He may have even chuckled a bit, though his voice was so soft and deep it was hard to tell. "Well said, Inspector, well said. Then policeman to policeman, tell me more about the case."

Ignoring the temptation to do a brief victory dance, McLean described the scene at #42 Farringdon Road as best he could. But even he found what he was saying hard to believe, and the idea there had been an "immaculate execution" faintly ludicrous. When he finished, Detective Motswagae was quiet for several minutes – though this time McLean found the lack of reaction vaguely reassuring.

"Inspector, I have never been to England, much less to Delacroix's London head office. Thus I cannot speak with authority about the security systems in that building. But here in Botswana diamonds are protected as carefully as life itself. If there is new technology to be had, we have it. If there are new techniques for spotting malfeasance, we use them. In the old days our security personnel met regularly with colleagues from America, Israel, Switzerland – anywhere that could teach us a trick or two. But these days the world comes to us. In fact, the US Government has just spent $60 million to buy our X-ray scanners for use at American airports. Since almost all of this technology was developed by Delacroix, I would assume that they take the same precautions we do – if not more – to protect their own property. I therefore find it extremely unlikely that two total strangers could enter the headquarters of Delacroix, unnoticed, and that one of them could kill the other – again without being seen."

"I share your skepticism, sir, I share it completely. Yet we do have a body which no one saw until the life had already drained out of him. You wanted to know why I'm in Gaborone? Here's the honest answer: it's the only lead I've got."

McLean paused for a moment, as the gears in his jet-lagged brain miraculously began to turn. "Detective, just now you said you thought it unlikely two total strangers could enter

#42 Farringdon Road unnoticed. Why did you think there were two of them?"

"I just assumed there would be a murderer and a victim. Perhaps it would have been more accurate to say 'at least two'."

"And why assume they were both strangers, when it's at least possible that either the murdered or the murderer worked for Delacroix and therefore had access to the building?"

Detective Motswagae looked at his fingernails, a sheepish smile appearing just briefly on his face. "Good catch, Inspector. I suppose I automatically assumed that a Delacroix employee would be above that sort of thing."

Now it was Inspector McLean's turn to sit quietly, unblinking eyes staring at his counterpart. Then he slid a piece of paper across the table.

"Here's a photo of the victim. Does he look at all familiar to you?"

Motswagae was silent – which McLean was beginning to think was the man's default mode – for several minutes. He appeared to be thinking hard, but whether searching his memory banks or coming up with a cover story was impossible to say. At last Motswagae exhaled loudly, and said, "No, I've never seen this man before in my life." Seeing that McLean was not satisfied with the response, Motswagae grudgingly continued. "Perhaps I should choose my words more carefully. As you know, Inspector, it's often hard to recognize people you don't know well from a picture of their lifeless bodies. So while I can't swear we've never met, I am absolutely certain I don't know who he is."

"If he had been involved with Delacroix or their joint venture here, what are the odds your paths would have crossed?"

"Probably very small. As you know, Delacroix is a private company – in terms of both ownership and corporate culture. They have to be, given the tremendous wealth concentrated in a diamond that can be easily stolen, easily transported and easily resold. Moreover the white community in Botswana is very small – mostly aid workers and the occasional expat working for a multinational. In general they mix with each other, not the locals, and spend time at the small number of hotels, bars and restaurants that could be considered up to international standards."

"Is there racial tension here?"

"Relations between blacks and whites are very good, not least because we remain thankful to Great Britain for making us a protectorate when apartheid South Africa wanted to absorb us into a sort of northern territory. But peaceful co-existence doesn't mean we spend a lot of time together."

"Why is that?"

"Money, mostly. The salaries enjoyed by expats are beyond the wildest imaginings of ordinary Batswana."

"Why such a difference?"

"Supposedly no one with the required skills and experience would be willing to come to Botswana if they were unable to have the same standard of living they had at home. That means larger, newer housing with every modern convenience. It means private schools – usually boarding schools across the border in South Africa – that European universities will acknowledge. It means doctors familiar with European bodies and diseases, as well as local health risks. All of that costs money."

"Would you say the Europeans are resented?"

"I think it would be more accurate to say that their wealth is resented. But Batswana know they need to learn the skills these people possess."

"Is there no place where the two worlds meet?"

"There is some overlap at restaurants, though the ones preferred by the expatriate community tend to be wildly overpriced. And restaurants aren't usually conducive to making new friends. Bars are better for that sort of thing, but I'm sad to say that while Botswana has avoided many of the pitfalls encountered by larger, richer nations, alcohol abuse isn't one of them. For financial reasons we tend to drink things expats rightfully find revolting."

McLean stifled a gasp of laughter.

"They are all very strong and very cheap," Detective Motswagae continued, sensing the Inspector's amusement. "The most popular is *bojalwa*, a sort of sorghum beer. We also have a homemade wine called *khadi*. And then there's the truly dangerous stuff. *Tho-tho-tho*, which translates as 'the dizzy spell', is over 80% alcohol. *A lala fa*, which translates as 'you sleep right there'. And *laela mmago*, which means 'say goodbye to your mother'."

McLean could contain his laughter no longer. "Those are some very poetic names for some very nasty sounding drinks."

"Wait until you taste them, Inspector. I'm not sure even the people who consume them regularly can claim to like them. But my point is that we drink different things than the expats, and that means we drink in different places."

"Do expats ever visit the local bars, just for the experience?"

"It's rare. Most of the local watering holes are really just shacks, called shebeen, and as the evening wears on they can become unpleasant and even dangerous places. Far too many Batswana men get their weekly wages on Friday, in cash, and head straight for the bars. And far too many will have drunk those wages – and then some – before they finally try to make their way home in the early hours of Saturday morning."

"And that means you spend your time dealing with fights, drunk drivers, destruction of property... that sort of thing."

"Precisely. And it also means our bars are not the sort of place a well-paid expat would want to visit."

"Ok. So the odds of someone having seen the victim before are practically non-existent. Let's talk about official records. What happens when someone enters the country? Do you photograph everyone at Immigration?"

"My understanding is that the Home Office looked at purchasing the necessary technology, but decided the cost couldn't be justified given the still small numbers of visitors to this country."

"Why so small?"

"Partly by choice. We decided to focus on high-value tourists who would bring money into the country without destroying the delicate balance between man and wildlife that attracts visitors in the first place. Inspector, if you have the time I strongly suggest you visit the Okavango. It's probably the only place left on earth where you can see not just the occasional elephant, giraffe or antelope grazing in the distance, but huge herds of a thousand or more animals. While Kenya is more famous, people who know say there is no better place in the world for a safari than Botswana."

"I certainly hope I have the opportunity to see for myself. But before I can start looking for elephants, I need to find a killer. And an identity for the victim."

"And you're assuming you'll find one – or both – of those here in Gaborone."

"Quite honestly, Detective Motswagae, I don't know where else to look.

CHAPTER 9

Johannesburg, January 7, 10:30 a.m.

Clifford Watkins was worried. For the last seven years he had been living not just one lie – but several. And now they were all about to come crashing down upon his head.

The man standing in front of him was at least 6'6", and probably 220 pounds – all of it muscle. He had the cauliflower ears and broken nose of a boxer, and his skin was tanned and wrinkled by spending too much time in the sun. An ugly scar running from just below his right ear to his collarbone looked like a knife wound. Add the blonde hair, and Clifford was almost certain this was one of those Afrikaners who farm, fight, and dream of a return to the days when Apartheid South Africa was a white man's paradise. Convinced they were the *victims* of genocide – as illustrated by the small number of Afrikaners who had been attacked by black gangs in recent years – they never went anywhere without a gun.

In this case it was a 9mm Glock, with a 17-shot magazine. This wasn't a gun one brandished to scare off an attacker; this was a gun for killing people.

"You could have gotten away with it, you know. It was a pretty good idea. And if you'd done – I don't know – maybe one stone a year, no one would have been the wiser. But your ego got the better of you, didn't it Clifford? You weren't content with just a little tom. You wanted to be *loaded.* And – here's the part that really screwed you, Cliffy – you wanted everyone to know it."

"I haven't the slightest idea what you're talking about."

"Sure you do, Clif-ford" the man said, mockingly stretching out the syllables. "I'm no Einstein, but even I can figure out how to fly this one below the radar. Sell one stone quietly in Antwerp. The next in Tel Aviv. Then one in Mumbai before going to New York or back to Antwerp. Use cut-outs, so no one knows where the diamonds are coming from. There's no pattern. Just a series of one-off deals with no questions asked. If you'd done it like that, you'd be sitting on top of the world instead of sitting here with me. But that's not you, is it my bru? You want to be noticed, the guy drinking Cristal in the VIP Room while all the sweet cherries with cut-rate boob jobs wonder who you are. And that's what makes you stupid."

"I resent that."

"Ain't nothing but the truth, Clifford. Otherwise I wouldn't be here."

"Well, since you brought it up, why *are* you here?"

"To remind you of some history. Our story begins in 2004 when Delacroix put the Orangevelt mine up for sale. She was a beauty in her day, they say, but by then she was pretty much tapped out. The Big Five all took a look, and not one

Johannesburg, January 7, 10:30 a.m.

of them made a bid. Said it's a dry hole. Any of that sound familiar, Cliffy?"

"It's public knowledge. Of course it sounds familiar."

"But then you come in, with a brand new company, and no experience running a mine, and put in an offer. A generous offer, seeing that you didn't need to outbid anyone. And less than two weeks later Delacroix announces you've won the auction *and* the sale has been concluded. I'm told that's pretty fast for that sort of thing."

"As you said, ours was the only offer on the table. Of course Delacroix said yes quickly; they were afraid we'd back out."

"I'm sure that's it. Of course. What other reason could there be? Anyhow, the guys who practically invented diamonds say there's nothing left worth having in that mine. Then you walk in, and nine months later you trip over a diamond the size of a melon. What did you sell it for, about $14 million?"

"About that, yes."

"Well aren't you just the luckiest bastard who ever walked the face of this earth? Delacroix spent 46 years in that mine and never saw a diamond bigger than a golf ball. Then you come in – your background is in sales, isn't it? – and this big-ass sparkler is just lying at your feet. Now tell me: what are the odds of that happening?"

"You've got to understand, we don't mine the same way as Delacroix. Their business is based on volume, so they set the crushers to break up the Kimberlite – that's the volcanic rock in which most diamonds are found -- into small pieces. We set the crushers so that the stones are left much bigger. That means we miss some of the small stuff, which we couldn't sell anyway. But we increase the odds of keeping large diamonds – like the 212-carater – intact. It's a different approach to mining based on two different business models."

The Afrikaner clapped his hands slowly, disdain falling from his fingertips like an ice cream cone dripping in the sun. "Bravo, Clifford, bravo. Everyone said you were clever. And I'm sure if you told that story to a class of first-year geology students they might actually believe it. But there are two problems with it. First, Delacroix said the mine had nothing left but small stones. So why would you come in and set the crushers on "Large"?

"It was done on the advice of our geologists, having concluded a thorough assay of the site."

"Say I accept that – which I don't, because it's clearly bullshit. But let's say I do and move on to Problem Two: how do you explain finding not just one large diamond – which could have been beginner's luck – but *13*, all in the first two years? And in a mine that produced just six decent-sized stones in the last *four decades*?"

"As I told you, we have a different business model than Delacroix. They make their money from volume; we make ours from a small number of large stones. Perhaps our approach gets a few more headlines, but that doesn't mean it's better. It's just different."

Johannesburg, January 7, 10:30 a.m.

"I see. Very helpful explanation. Clears everything up nicely." The man paused, cracked his knuckles loudly, and stuck his face six inches from Clifford's nose. "There's just one last thing. If crusher settings are the secret of your success, why haven't you found a single large diamond since your IPO three years ago? You made close to $1.5 *billion* from that deal, thanks to a stock price inflated by all those megarocks you found. But since you cashed out, all you've found is pebbles. Don't you find that just the least bit suspicious?"

"But that's the way this business works! Mining for diamonds is an art, not a science. No one can tell you where the stones are hidden, or how big they are, or when you'll find them. It's more about luck than skill."

"And your luck ran out on the day you became a billionaire. That's the story you're asking me to swallow, Clifford?"

"I'm telling you that the output of a mine – any mine – varies from day to day. No one, not even Delacroix, can predict today with any great accuracy what size and quality of diamond is going to be found tomorrow. We had a good run in the beginning, followed by a quiet period. But over the long term I remain confident an investment in our company is a wise investment."

The man looked to his right, and then his left, and then directly back at Clifford. "Just hunting for the teleprompter. Or did you memorize that little speech?"

"Have faith. I'm sure we will find more large stones in the future."

"Perhaps you will. But in the mean time you're sitting on a large pile of money that doesn't belong to you. You see, my employer thinks maybe you planted those large stones in order to make a worthless hole in the ground look like a valuable diamond mine so you could flog it off to people you take for suckers. You make a fortune, get your picture in the paper, and have people saying you beat the mighty Delacroix at their own game. Meanwhile, my boss gets to watch his investment turn to shit."

"And who might that boss be?"

"I don't think that's important, Clifford. Surely you want to ensure *all* of your stakeholders are satisfied, don't you?"

With that the Afrikaner tapped his gun, winked, and left the office.

As the door shut, Clifford thought he was going to faint. His breath was short and rapid, and his heart felt like it was trying to jump out of his chest. He had always been afraid of bullies; bullies carrying a gun, in a city where people get shot in broad daylight for looking at someone the wrong way, terrified him. Clifford took several deep breaths, and wiped the sweat off his forehead. He went over to the bar, took out a Baccarat glass and poured himself a generous helping of Lagavulin. He swallowed it in one go. And then he smiled. He was happy to be alive and unhurt. But he was even happier that the Afrikaner – who knew a lot more than he should – appeared to know nothing about the only secret Clifford truly cared about.

CHAPTER 10

Johannesburg, March 18, 2:15 a.m.

"Inspector?"

"Huh?"

"Inspector, it's me, Thomas, sir."

"Why are you calling me in the middle of the night?"

"The time difference, sir."

"Thomas, you're an idiot. There's only an hour's difference between London and Gaborone."

"Oh. I didn't know that. I'll remember next time, sir, I promise. But sir..."

"But what? Whatever it is had better be pretty damn important."

"It's the autopsy report. It just came back and I thought you'd like to know right away."

"Thomas, I saw the bullet hole. I can figure out what that means."

"That's just it sir."

"What's it, Thomas?"

"The gunshot, sir. It was post-mortem."

"Dead men don't bleed, Watkins, and I saw the corpse lying in a pool of blood."

"That's what I'm trying to tell you, sir. The blood wasn't the victim's."

"What?"

"It wasn't the victim's blood. But that's not the strangest part."

"Much as I hate to admit it, Thomas, now you've got my attention. Whose blood is it?"

"It isn't."

The Inspector found himself thinking of Alice stepping through the looking glass, and had nothing to say for a good fifteen seconds. Then: "What do you mean 'it isn't'?"

"It isn't human. It's pig's blood."

"*Pig's blood!* Are you absolutely sure?"

"The lab triple-checked."

"So how did he die? And why was his body dumped in a lake of pig's blood?"

"Doc says it was a heart attack, probably 4-5 hours before the body was discovered."

"So you're telling me the victim snuck into the most secure building in Europe, carrying..." – the Inspector found it difficult even to say the words, they were so absurd – "a bucket of pig's blood; was seen by absolutely no one; had a fatal heart attack but before dying managed to pour the blood on the floor in such a way that it looked like the blood had come from him; then he artfully lay down in the blood and died of that protracted heart attack, and then, by God, he shot himself."

"That's certainly what it looks like, sir."

"You're an idiot, Thomas. A complete and total idiot."

The Inspector hung up the phone, lay back in bed, and considered the question of whether Thomas had been the only idiot on the call.

CHAPTER 11

Gaborone, March 18, 7:30 a.m.

By the time Inspector McLean gave up trying to sleep it was already 90 degrees, the sun so bright it made his eyes throb. As he dragged himself out of bed he was certain that airline seats were an invention of the devil. It didn't matter if one sat up straight, or slouched, or curled up in a little ball; there was simply no way to sit in them that didn't result in agonizing lower back pain by the time the wheels touched down, and the pain got exponentially worse the following day. The four hours' sleep he got last night on a thin but lumpy mattress had added insult to injury. As he stood in the shower hoping the weak spray of warm water would coax his aching muscles to loosen up, he thought about all those people in his office who said they envied him his big African adventure. Little did they know that international business travel is mostly about too little sleep and near-constant intestinal distress.

Plus back pain.

What an old grouch I'm getting to be, he thought grumpily.

He stumbled down to the breakfast room and ordered coffee. As the caffeine began to work its magic, he realized he was hungry. Fortunately the breakfast buffet at the

Mokolwane Bistro looked promising – a mix of western, Indian and local specialties. McLean put a little of everything on his plate, figuring he'd sample them all and then go back for generous helpings of whichever options tasted best. After polishing off the eggs, bacon and a surprisingly nice vegetable curry, he sat back in his chair with his coffee in one hand and his case notes in the other.

One John Doe. Approximate age: 60-65. Nationality: unknown. Country of residence: unknown. Died of a heart attack before being shot – unseen – in the most secure facility in Europe. Found lying in a pool of pig's blood. Open and shut case, really.

He ordered more coffee.

Only clue is a note saying REMEMBER GABORONE. However, here in Gaborone, no one has a clue what the clue means. Local police polite but not particularly helpful. Say there has never been a war or other historical incident to which the clue might be referring. Race relations reasonably good, though some class tensions. Delacroix clearly rules the roost, but keeps to itself. Excellent security systems, which is why what happened at #42 Farringdon Road should not have happened.

But, of course, it did. And that left Inspector McLean without the foggiest notion of where to go from here.

He postponed the decision by having some toast with imported English thick-cut marmalade.

What happened in Gaborone that's supposed to be remembered? Did anything happen here? *Does* anything happen

Gaborone, March 18, 7:30 a.m.

here? It wouldn't seem so, judging from how quiet the casino was last night when he walked around the grounds for a post-prandial stroll.

No, the only action in town was the diamond giant. And that got McLean thinking about yesterday's meeting with Detective Motswagae. At no point did he mention that Delacroix had flown someone in to meet with him, which would seem to be a highly relevant point under the circumstances. Maybe that was McLean's fault. If he'd asked the question, would it have been answered? Or was the detective under orders to stay as silent about the company as it was about itself?

On the other hand, perhaps the detective was just doing what coppers do: offering up no more than they have to, hoping the guy on the other side of the table would reveal something useful. Zipped lips were an occupational hazard, one that nearly cost McLean his marriage. For years Edith had waited up for him, hoping to be entertained with true crime stories while she sipped her Chardonnay and watched him eat his congealed supper. And every night he sat there in stony silence, his mind still racing through the events of the day while his mouth did nothing but chew. He simply couldn't face the silly questions he knew she'd ask, or her feeble attempts to solve his mysteries for him. Instead he just watched as his marriage began to fray, and Edith started ordering her Chardonnay by the case.

"Maybe I'll ask Motswagae how they handle the domestic front in Botswana," McLean said laughingly to the empty room. "After all, there's got to be *something* that man will talk about." But trading tips on marital bliss would have to wait. Right now he needed a plan of action for the day ahead. For lack of a better alternative, McLean decided to do exactly what he'd told Chief Franklin he was going to do: shake the tree over at Delacroix.

Being ever so careful, of course, not to upset that nice Mr. Weil. Wouldn't want to worry the Queen.

It was time to get on with it. McLean ordered more coffee.

The Queen. Delacroix certainly does have friends in high places. Wonder if the same is true here in Botswana. Probably – diamonds are a much higher percentage of Botswana's GDP than they are the UK's. Maybe someone resented the company's political clout? Or maybe it had taken some of its friends in government for granted, and was being sent a none-too-gentle reminder to REMEMBER GABORONE?

The fact was, McLean could sit here all day pulling conspiracy theories out of thin air. But the chances of any of them being even partially correct were pretty slim. As Chief Franklin had always said, "when in doubt – get out". Start banging on doors and see what happens. It may not be an inspired plan, but it was the only one he had.

Inspector McLean left most of the coffee in the cup, signed the check, and left.

CHAPTER 12

Antwerp, January 6, 11:15 a.m.

It hadn't been easy for Daniel to raise $1.5 million in cash. While his credit was good, he'd never borrowed anything close to that much money. The bankers might believe he stumbled across a once-in-a-lifetime opportunity, but for a loan that big they'd need to see the diamonds. Maybe ask for proof he had customers lined up. And when they compared the 138-carater with the price he was paying for it, they'd know he'd gotten a steal.

Literally.

So going to the bankers was out of the question. The official bankers, that is.

He knew, he simply *knew* the smart move was just to walk away. Instead he went to see a man everyone spoke about, but no one admitted to actually doing business with. His name was Achmed Khalif. A Lebanese trader and "unofficial banker", Khalif claimed to specialize in diamonds, but there were rumors he had nice little sidelines in money laundering, gun running, and heroin. Daniel would have given odds Khalif would refuse to see him, but as an attractive secretary escorted him into Khalif's tastefully furnished office he was greeted like an old friend.

"Ah, Mr. Stern! I woke up this morning with a feeling today was going to be a good day for business... and now here you are, right on cue!"

"Good morning to you, sir. Um, I was hoping to see you about, um..."

"You need money."

"How did you know?"

"Sir, that's the only reason anyone calls upon a humble trader such as myself. Mr. Stern – might I be permitted to call you 'Daniel'?"

"Uh, sure. Of course."

"Daniel, I have been in business in this same spot for 21 years. Before that my father – may his soul rest in peace – sat in this very chair for 46 years. Over the course of those seven decades we have seen thousands of men cross our threshold, and have developed a sort of skill – a knack, that's the word! – for recognizing their needs."

"Well, that's great. Would you like to hear why I need the money?"

"Of course not, my dear Daniel! I am certain you would not be asking without a very good reason. And I am equally certain that whatever you invest in will enable you to pay me back promptly."

"Yes, speaking of that... what are your terms for a loan of $1.5 million?"

"Daniel, would I be correct in thinking you are a fellow member of the diamond trade?"

"Um, yes. How did you know?"

"The calluses on your thumb and forefinger suggest you often handle diamonds using a pair of tweezers." Khalid paused, waiting for Daniel to look at his right hand. "Also, the ID card around your neck identifying you as a member of the Diamond Bourse was a bit of a hint."

"How stupid of me."

"Daniel, if you're borrowing money to buy rough diamonds, you'll have all the collateral I require. If you can pay back the principle with interest, I'm a happy man. If you pay back part of the money in cash, and the rest in diamonds, I'm happy. In fact, the only scenario in which I'm at all unhappy is if you were to take the money and disappear off the face of the earth. But a man of principle such as yourself wouldn't do that, would you, Daniel?"

The words were spoken lightly, with a touch of warmth. But there was something in Achmed's eyes that made Daniel's blood run cold. No threat had been uttered, but one was received loud and clear.

And then Daniel realized: He *knows*. Achmed knows exactly why I'm here. And once again he wished he had the strength to simply walk away.

"Now, Daniel, can I have the bank information for the recipient of these funds?"

"Actually, I need the money in cash."

"That's a rather... *unusual* arrangement."

"The seller has a bit of a cash flow problem. I got an excellent deal on the grounds I would pay them in cash."

"I see. Might we be permitted to wire the money to your account? You could then get the cash from your bank."

"I'd rather not involve them if at all possible. They might, um, get a little jealous I had come to you for the loan rather than to them."

"How very perceptive of you, Daniel. Please don't mistake my love of orderly processes and paperwork for a lack of enthusiasm. We want to do business with you, and if it is cash you want it is cash you shall have."

"Thank you. How long will it take to get the money?"

"No longer than it will take you to savor one of our excellent cups of coffee. We are inordinately proud of our espresso, though you could be forgiven for choosing the latte instead. What is your pleasure?"

"The latte, please. That will give you a little more time to pull that much money together."

"You are a very thoughtful man, Daniel Stern. I am sure we will have a long, enjoyable and mutually profitable business relationship from this day forward."

Despite the apparent sincerity of the sentiment, Daniel was most uncomfortable. His usual bank wouldn't have $1.5 million in cash sitting around on the off chance someone would come in requesting actual money rather than a wire transfer. And despite his nearly 20-year relationship with them, they wouldn't give him cash without asking a lot of questions. Cash usually meant someone didn't want to leave a trace, and while sometimes that was necessary when dealing with ultra-wealthy recluses, more often it was a bright red neon sign of shady dealing.

Were under-the-counter deals far more common than he knew? Or had Achmed been told in advance not only that Daniel would be coming, but that he would be requesting cash? If so, *who* told him?

The only person Daniel could think of was Frans – the tall, scary blonde man with a South African accent who was selling him the stone. Until now, Daniel had assumed the beast was totally ignorant about the industry and its key players. Now he was starting to worry whether the man knew far more than he should.

The latte was, as promised, excellent. Rich and creamy, yet the slightly bitter taste of the coffee still shone through. And, as promised, $1.5 million was placed in front of Daniel before he reached the bottom of the cup.

CHAPTER 13

London, 16 Years Earlier

Clifford Watkins was born in Seaford, England, the third son of a successful underwriter for Lloyds. Like his father before him, he was sent to a Scottish boarding school at the tender age of eight. His parents told him it would make him a man, toughen him up, teach him how to fend for himself. And it was true that the loneliness, the cold, the gloom and the dour professors had all worked together to make Clifford into the stiff-lipped man of few words whose *gravitas* was more shyness than serenity.

The school had another, equally profound effect on the boy. Except on the occasional weekend when the students were allowed to venture into town, Clifford had only two women in his life. One was the wife of the headmaster, a stern, irritable lady who preferred cats to human company. The other was his scout – a young Polish girl who cleaned his room each morning. She was no beauty; even the generous would find it difficult to describe her as merely "plump". So like so many before him, when the pounding of his hormones could no longer be ignored he experimented not with the fairer sex but with a boy two years his junior. Clifford didn't find the experience pleasurable, or even all that interesting. It was just something he needed to do.

After graduating from Balliol College Oxford he agreed to meet with a friend of his father's who worked for Delacroix in London. He knew going in the "chat" was really a job interview, and he had absolutely no interest in working for the firm. While his tastes ran more to fashion than finance, someone of his breeding *belonged* in banking – not in a mining company whose roots lay in the rough-and-tumble world of apartheid South Africa.

But something strange happened as he walked through the doors of #42 Farringdon Road. He felt as if he'd been allowed inside the ultimate club, a sort of secret society that people on the outside could only wonder about. As he clipped on the Visitors Badge that let him pass through the electronic doors like a member of staff, he felt special. Important. Chosen.

And he loved it.

He was led up to the ninth floor, and caught a glimpse of the massive Board Room – with its 20-foot long oak table – on his way to a smaller room where lunch would be served by the company's executive chef. The meal began with a cocktail, followed by white wine and an overly generous serving of grilled Scottish salmon. As the meat course was being served – together with an excellent Bordeaux -- the family friend asked briefly about Clifford's experience and goals. However he paid only minimal attention to the answers before launching into an enthusiastic introduction of the company's operations in far-away places with names out of a storybook. The Congo. Angola. Namibia. Tanzania. Botswana. Sierra Leone. Liberia. Zimbabwe.

Clifford had a vague recollection of hearing about those countries as a schoolboy, though odds were he couldn't find any of them on a map. But it was their very obscurity that grabbed hold of him and wouldn't let go. Just saying those romantic names sent his mind racing into Fantasy Land. Suddenly he saw himself as Lawrence of Arabia, crossing borders in the dark of night in order to carry out his mission, a confidante of both dictators and impoverished peasants, a raconteur with no equal. It was, he told himself, what he was born to do.

"Yes," he said.

"Yes what?"

"Yes, I'll take the job."

"But I haven't offered you one."

"Not yet, you haven't. But I assume that's merely a formality."

The family friend smiled. Mission accomplished.

Two weeks later, Clifford arrived at #42 Farringdon Road to begin his training. The first few hours were spent filling out forms and having the company rules and regulations read to him by a low-level HR person with a voice that would put even an insomniac to sleep. The real work began in the afternoon, with the first lecture on diamonds.

As Clifford and his new colleagues ambled into the training room, they saw a short, barrel-chested man with the florid nose of a habitual drinker and a scowl that seemed to suggest its owner derived great pleasure from being surly.

He was sitting on a desk at the front of the room, not saying a word; he just stared at his charges until they were all seated and silent. He then took a deep, dramatically painful breath, and began.

"My name is Jonnie White, Mr. White to you lot. Over the next two months I'm going to tell you what you need to know to make money for the company. Some of you will pay attention, learn a thing or two, and have a decent career. Some of you will think there's nothing an east London boy like me could possibly tell you. You'll spend the next eight weeks dreaming about the new secretary on the sales floor, who even I admit is a bit of all right. But trust me: a day will come when you wish you'd listened to Old Jonnie, as what I'm about to tell you might save your life.

"Or at least your job.

"I know most of you went to Uni, and are therefore the best and the brightest this nation has to offer. Don't worry: I'll speak slowly. Now, do any of you geniuses know where diamonds come from – and the first person to say "a jewelry store" gets to wash the teacups?"

Silence.

"Well, at least you're honest. Diamonds came from 90 miles below the surface of the earth, the mantle if you're taking notes. That's the only place with the heat and pressure needed to change carbon to diamond. We're talking temperatures of 2,000 degrees Fahrenheit, and 50,000 – 70,000 atmospheres of pressure.

London, 16 years Earlier

"Only once in the history of... everything did those conditions exist. And that's while the earth was cooling, 3.3 billion years ago. That's hundreds of millions of years before the first plants. A long, long time ago.

"Chances of ever seeing those conditions again? Zero. In other words, Mother Nature is out of the diamond business. Think about that. Every diamond that will ever be made has *already* been made. All that's left for us to do is find them.

"Now, if those diamonds had stayed down in the mantle, no one would have seen or heard of them. But fortunately for us, they managed to find a bus service to the earth's surface. Anyone know what it's called?"

Silence.

"And I thought you chaps were meant to know a thing or two. It's called the volcano. Volcanoes spat diamonds out of the center of the earth to where we've got a shot at finding them. Some of them made it all the way to the surface. Over time rain washes them towards the ocean, where we happily scoop them up. But most got trapped in volcanic rock called Kimberlite – for extra credit on the test, remember it's named after the city of Kimberley where your esteemed employers got their start – and have to be set free.

"That's the job of the boys in Mining. They get to dig up huge amounts of Kimberlite, break it into little chunks, and pray they're not breaking the diamonds while they're at it. To find just one carat of diamond they need to dig up, transport, crush and sort 250 *tons* of Kimberlite. Tell that to any anorak-wearing smart ass who says diamonds aren't rare.

"You'll get a chance to see some actual mining when we send you down the Big Hole in Kimberley. I would recommend you wear an adult diaper, because you're going to shit yourselves when you're standing underneath a mile of solid rock and the boys set off a truckload of dynamite. But that's a pleasure for another day. Today I want you to focus on just how difficult it is to find a mine – any mine – in the first place.

"To locate Kimberlite we look for what's called an indicator stone, the most reliable of which is garnet. If you find garnet, there's maybe a 1 in 1,000 chance you've found a diamond pipe. We have 20 people in Jo'burg who spend all day every day looking at what you and I would call sand – one grain at a time – hoping to find a garnet. And most of them will complete their entire careers without ever finding a diamondiferous pipe.

"Even when you do come good on a 1,000 to 1 shot, the work is just beginning. Only 1 in 100 diamond-bearing pipes has enough diamond to make it *potentially* commercially viable. And making that determination requires several more years of work, mostly in the form of cutting huge slices of solid rock and bringing them back to Johannesburg where they can be smashed into little pieces which are then examined one at a time by men and women working with tweezers and magnifying glasses. Whatever they find gets weighed and sorted by quality, allowing the bean counters to work their magic and come up with an estimate of the mine's potential value. Mining then does their own calculations on the cost of getting those diamonds out of the ground. Then management compares the two sets of numbers, and

London, 16 Years Earlier

decides whether or not to make a multi-*billion* dollar bet on what's really just an educated guess.

"So how often does a new mine come into being? Well, Delacroix spends over $100 million dollars a year trying to find new mines. Guess how many we've found?"

Various numbers were thrown out in voices lacking confidence but attempting nonetheless to convey enthusiasm.

"Five? You in the back, are you willing to go higher than that? 10? That's a brave boy. Of course, it's also a boy who is totally and completely wrong. In the last 25 years Delacroix – the acknowledged expert in everything to do with diamonds – has found exactly *one* major new mine."

The room was so silent you could hear dust falling.

"If you take just one thing out of today's session, let it be this: it's not easy to make money in diamonds. Surprised? If you're like the average punter, you assumed that because diamonds are expensive they must be hugely profitable. You thought Delacroix executives spend their days deciding which glamorous Hollywood star to hang out with next. You thought the company was printing money, and didn't have to work for a living like the other poor sods. Well, lads, you were wrong. Anyone who tells you it's easy to make money in diamonds is ignorant, lying, or stealing from someone else. The core of this business – the part without which none of the rest can happen – is dirty, difficult, dangerous, and nearly impossible for anyone who lacks our knowledge and expertise. So a few months from now when you're having a two-hour lunch with a customer at company expense, spare a thought for the people sifting through grains of sand one by one in search of a tiny speck of garnet. Raise your glass to the guys who set off explosions that could leave them buried underground. Say a word of thanks to the guys who drive trucks across roads in northern Canada made of nothing but ice, a journey so terrifying that one-third of the drivers have to be flown out because they can't face the drive back. Think about all of these people and thank them for what they do, because without them none of you would be here."

Jonnie White looked around the room, and saw every one of his charges was looking pale and sheepish. He had taken a room full of Britain's best and brightest, and made them feel unworthy to kiss his feet. The morning's training session was a complete and total success.

CHAPTER 14

Gaborone, March 18, 10:15 a.m.

A surprisingly invigorated McLean smiled at the sad and still deserted gift shop, and went out the front entrance of the hotel in search of a taxi. While none was waiting, it didn't take more than 10 minutes for yet another battered white Toyota to make a noisy appearance. As he squeezed his rather large frame into the undersized car, McLean ordered the driver to take him to Delacroix.

"Which one?"

"There's more than one?"

"Oh, yes. Too many to count, my friend. There's Delacroix International, Delacroix Botswana, Delacroix Diamond Mining, Delacroix Diamond Trading, Delacroix Diamond Development, and…"

"What's the difference?"

"Who knows? It seems like they set up a new company every other day."

"Why would they do that?"

"To hide all the money they are making from Botswana diamonds!" The driver laughed in a rich, resonant baritone that brought a smile to McLean's usually dour face.

"I thought your government had a joint venture with Delacroix."

"Oh, they do, they do. But who knows what goes on between the two of them. All I know is that no one has ever handed me a large stack of money and said 'Here, Good Citizen, is your share of your nation's diamond wealth".

"Surely the money goes into building schools and roads and that sort of thing?"

"That's what they tell us. But how do we know that Delacroix is playing fair with us? How do we know they're not underpaying us for our diamonds, and then selling them in New York or London for a massive profit?"

"You're asking the wrong man. I'm just an ordinary copper." McLean thought for a minute. "But can't you just look at what a diamond sells for at your local jeweler, and compare that price with what the government is giving Delacroix?"

The driver laughed out loud again. "I have lived here in Gabs my entire life, and do you know how many diamonds I've seen? Not one. Not one single diamond. Doesn't that strike you as strange? And do you know something else? The great nation of Botswana, the world's #1 producer of diamonds, doesn't have any jewelry stores. Can you believe that?"

"No, actually, I can't. Why is that?"

"The only rich people in this country work for Delacroix. If they need a diamond, they just reach into their giant vaults and take one."

"What does the government say about that?"

"Nothing. They don't have to. The same party has been in power since Independence in 1967, and will probably remain in power until my great-great-great grandchildren have gray hair and no teeth."

The Toyota wheezed and rumbled on.

"I thought Botswana was a democracy."

"That's certainly the theory. But the opposition has no money, whereas the ruling party has mountains of it. They simply outspend the competition, telling us how much better they've made the lives of ordinary Batswana."

"You don't agree with that?"

"Life *is* better, there's no doubt about that. But that's because of our diamonds. Without those, the ruling party could have done nothing. With them, even the opposition could be effective."

"Do you wonder if Delacroix is propping up the current government to ensure they can continue to operate in a favorable environment?"

"I wonder many things, but I know nothing at all. Maybe you can find out. I'll take you to the new Delacroix Diamond Trading building so you can ask them for me." The driver again let loose an ironic, almost mocking laugh. "Can you believe it: that one building cost $67 million. $67 million! You could buy most of Botswana for that much money. Now tell me: why does anyone need a building like that, just to go to work?"

A few minutes later the Toyota pulled up in front of what McLean had to admit was a very impressive building.

"This is as far as I go, sir. The guards may shoot me if I try to drive you to the entrance." The statement was punctuated by yet another hardy laugh, but McLean had to wonder whether the man was really joking.

McLean got out of the cab, pulled his badge and warrant card out of his jacket pocket, and walked briskly towards the guard tower. In reply, the guards adjusted their AK-47's.

"Hello. I am Inspector McLean of the London Metropolitan Police Force. I would like to speak to someone in charge."

"Do you have an appointment?"

"No, but I'm sure your boss will make time for a representative of Her Majesty's Government." The Metropolitan Police actually work for the mayor of London, not the Queen. But McLean figured even the police are entitled to stretch the truth occasionally.

"I'm sorry, Inspector, but for security reasons we cannot admit anyone who isn't on the list. And without an appointment, you're not on the list."

"I've explained..."

"Inspector, I'm going to have to ask you to leave. Now."

The AK-47's moved closer to the firing position.

McLean looked back over his shoulder, and saw to his immense relief that the taxi hadn't moved. In fact, the driver seemed to be enjoying the little drama unfolding before his eyes, as well as the expectation of a return fare. "Take you back if you like," he said.

Wordlessly, McLean crawled back into the cab.

Damn. Frontal assault didn't work. Maybe it's deliberate obstruction, or maybe you really can't just walk into what's probably the most secure building in the whole country.

Most secure building in the country. Just like #42 Farringdon Road. You can't get in unless you're inside already.

Like a bolt out of the blue, McLean suddenly realized he'd been approaching this all wrong. Blame the heat. Blame the pain in his back. Blame the AK-47's. "Take me back to the Grand Palm, as fast as you can go!"

When he got back to his room, he called Thomas.

"Hello, sir. How's the weather there?"

"Light snow flurries and the promise of an overnight blizzard. Thomas, it's Africa. It's hot and dry. Every single day."

"Oh. Right, sir. Sorry, sir. How can I help you?"

"Thomas, I want you to call that chap who runs Delacroix, Something Something Weil. Tell him I want an all-access pass. Carte blanche. Every facility they've got down here. Tell him if he doesn't open the doors I'll hold a press conference via Skype and inform the British public that a murder investigation is being blocked by 'unnamed senior executives' at Delacroix."

"Certainly, sir. But doesn't that seem a bit, um, *aggressive*?"

"I need to make some progress before the snow storms close all the roads." And with that, Inspector McLean hung up on a most mystified Thomas.

CHAPTER 15

London and the Democratic Republic of the Congo

"Before we begin, are there any questions from yesterday?"

One brave fool in the back raised his hand. "In the hallway there's a picture of a diamond set in black rock. Is that what the miners are looking for?"

"Only when doing their Christmas shopping. First off, the sparkler in that photo is a polished diamond. And while Mother Nature gives us many things, a pre-cut and polished diamond isn't one of them. Second, most people who work in the mines will *never* see a single diamond, even if they spend 30 years looking. I've clearly failed to convey to you just how rare diamonds are, and how hard it is to wrest them from the bowels of the earth. It's not like picking mushrooms in the forest. Besides, that photo is a composite – the sort of sleight of hand at which the boffins in Marketing excel." The lecturer paused. "Does that answer your question?"

A submissive nod of the head suggested the affirmative.

"Right." White paused just long enough to ensure that was it for this morning's allotment of asinine questions. "Yesterday we talked about the fairly minute chances of finding any diamonds in the first place – or at least *I* did. Today we're going to assume that you've got yourself a mine, and it is producing – and bear in mind not all of them do. What happens next?"

The lecturer waited for a beat or two.

"You count up what you've got. Sounds easy, right? Wrong. First you've got to sort the diamonds. By weight, which we measure in carats." White paused, preparing to trot out the very same joke he had used at this exact point in every introductory lecture he'd given for the past 17 years. "But this has nothing to do with Bugs Bunny."

For the seventeenth straight year, no one laughed.

White gave a bit of a wry smile, a warning that the next time he made a joke they had better find it hilarious. And then he pressed ahead. "Instead it comes from the weight of a carob bean: a fifth of a gram. Next you sort by color. Then by clarity. Then shape. We'll be spending two full weeks teaching you how to do that, and even then you won't be very good at it. In fact, if even one of you is able to achieve 50% accuracy by the end of the fortnight, we'll leave an hour early and I'll buy a round of drinks at the pub. Hell, make it two; one can afford to proffer a generous offer when there's absolutely no chance of having to make good on it."

"Part of the reason this is so difficult is the specificity we demand. Delacroix sorts diamonds into more than 12,000 different groups, each of which is priced differently. And that price changes every eight weeks. Fortunately you don't have to worry about pricing until next month; for now I just want you to imagine how infinitesimal the variation is between the different groups, and how difficult it is to be able to spot that variation, consistently, day after day, week after week, and year after year.

"But you're not home and dry yet. For after we sell the rough diamonds, they are cut and polished, and then sorted again. You'll be spending a week learning how that process is done, even though Delacroix isn't involved with polish. Why, you say? Because the price of rough is very dependent on the price of the polish that comes out of it. And you lot won't be able to sell the rough that pays for Mr. Hamilton's lovely new tie – shall we all turn to look at him and admire his new cravat for just a moment? – unless you can convince your customers it is priced fairly given the polish that's likely to result.

"Oh, yes. With polish there's a fourth dimension: cut. That involves some math, some geometry, and a practiced eye I doubt any of you will develop while I'm still alive. Something to look forward to then."

Jonnie White had to work hard to keep a smile off his face. This was the part of working in The Diamond Training Centre that he absolutely loved. Unlike the pasty-faced twits he had now scared into submission, White had never gone to university, joining the diamond trade as an apprentice polisher at the age of 18. Like so many graduates of The School of the Street, he was smart, tough and resourceful – but not destined for the life of glamor and privilege his young charges would eventually enjoy. That didn't bother him overly much; he found tormenting his "betters" kept him a reasonably happy man.

Yet there was at least one man in the room who found the difficulty and complexity of the task ahead to be truly exhilarating. As Clifford Watkins took furious notes, he realized he'd always assumed diamonds were simple: dig 'em up, whack 'em in some jewelry, and sell 'em to Tiffany's for a fortune. That would be a nice business model, but a boring career. Spending his life playing Treasure Hunt with Mother Nature sounded infinitely more enjoyable. So did developing expertise in a very obscure area with which he could impress his friends. So when Jonnie White packed his young charges off to the Rough Division to spend two weeks actually sorting diamonds, Clifford found himself in the grip of something quite unusual for a middle class Brit: excitement.

It didn't last long. Weighing the stones was easy enough: just drop them on a scale that measures carats down to five digits to the right of the decimal point, and you're done. Color, however, was a bit harder. Even experienced sorters found it difficult to look at a single diamond and pronounce its color. Instead they would compare each diamond to be evaluated with a Master Set until they had found a position for the stone in which it was darker than the sample stone on its left, but lighter than the one on its right. It wasn't hard work... at least for the first 20 minutes or so. But after that Clifford found his eyes began to glaze over, and all of the stones looked exactly the same. Or completely different. Or different this time than the last time he looked. How anyone managed to do this eight hours a day, five days a week was completely beyond him.

But even color sorting was easy compared to quality. Most diamonds contain black specks – bits of carbon not fully converted to diamond – called inclusions. The problem is, depending on how you look at a stone those inclusions may or may not be visible. There is an art to looking *through* the stone with both eyes fully open, and then rotating it slowly so that imperfections invisible from only one angle suddenly pop into view.

The instructors in the Rough Division were able to spot inclusions almost instantaneously; by the end of the week Clifford could do a reasonable job in just over 20 minutes. But more often than not, when it came time to check his work he learned he'd overlooked at least one flaw in more than half the diamonds he was given – and in some cases two or three. Do the same thing out in the field, and he would end up overpaying for every diamond he bought.

The worst part, however, was that he was rarely able to generate the same result twice. To test himself he'd look at the same stone first thing in the morning and last thing at night. Not once during the two-week training period did his morning self agree with his evening self. He was therefore pleased when Rough Training was finally finished, and they were sent across the street to the Polish division. The work on carat, color and quality was the same, and Clifford felt his damaged confidence rise just a bit. But Polish also introduced the idea of Cut. There are machines that can measure the proportions of a cut diamond, and compare that with the specifications for an "ideal" diamond. But it didn't take too long before it was clear to the entire class that two diamonds with the same technical measurements could look very different, and that the only truly reliable guide to cut quality was the human eye. Days were then spent balancing diamonds on the "v" where the first and second fingers come together, then moving the hand ever-so-slightly so light would hit the stone at different angles. As he watched the diamond's sparkle dance, jump and dive, Clifford was transfixed.

Six weeks after the training began, the lecturer announced the technical section of the training was complete. Now it was time to apply that background knowledge to the serious business of turning rough rocks into shiny ones, and shiny ones into money.

"For *diamantaires* – the people who cut and polish diamonds -- the difference between vast wealth and bankruptcy lies in the yield: the percentage of a rough stone that is successfully converted into polished diamond. And that yield varies greatly depending on the type of rough diamond being cut.

"The most profitable is a Sawable Dodecahedron, which looks like two pyramids lined up based to base. Cut it in half and round the edges, and you're well on your way to having two Round Brilliant diamonds. The process is so efficient the yield is 50% or more.

"Ordinary Sawables look like Dodecahedrons that have been banged up a bit. It can still be cut in half to create two stones that look something like a finished diamond. But because of its irregular shape yields drop to the low 40's. That's better than a Makeable – which looks like a cloudy, misshapen ice cube – or a Flat, which looks like a piece of a broken glass bottle. Often less than 30% of these stones ends up in a finished diamond. And the less one says about Maccles the better.

"As you might imagine, Dodecahedrons are far more expensive than Makeables. But that doesn't mean they're necessarily more popular. In fact, because it's so much easier to convert a Dodecahedron to polish efficiently, any decent diamond cutter can do it. And as I'm sure all you bright young things remember from your Introductory Economics class at university, when barriers to entry are low, so are margins. On the other hand, there are only a handful of companies that specialize in Makeables, and while theirs is a less glamorous end of the business, the margins are usually very attractive. Your job, then, is to match horses with courses, ensuring that the right goods get into the right hands so that yields are maximized across the board and everyone goes home at the end of the day exceedingly rich."

Clifford raised his hand. "Surely in today's world there are technological solutions to the problems of these more complex diamonds?"

The lecture smiled – or smirked: his charges often found it hard to tell the difference. "That is actually a very astute question. I may go to the dog races tonight while my luck holds. Yes, Mr. Watkins, it's now possible to cut even the most complicated diamond structures using lasers. Anyone want to hazard a guess as to why these machines are not used with *all* diamond cutting?"

"They're too expensive?" came a tentative voice from the back of the room.

"No. Well, yes, they *are* expensive. Even if you buy from the Chinese a single machine will set you back more than $1 million, but that's not the reason they're used only for the most difficult stones. What does a laser do? Anyone? It burns through things. Unfortunately that process results in about 1-2% of the diamond being lost. And since *diamantaires* usually operate with a margin of 7-12%, that's a considerable portion of your profit going up – quite literally – in smoke. As I've been saying repeatedly for the past two days – all together, if you'd be so kind – *it's all about the yield.*"

Abandoning caution, Clifford raised his hand a second time. "If a 1-2% loss rate has that big an impact on profitability, isn't it even more important to get the price of the rough stone right in the first place?"

"Goodness me, there is hope for the younger generation!" White said in a drawl that might have been an Englishman's impression of an American southern accent. "Yes, in a low-margin business you have to get your price – both buying and selling – absolutely right. And a few months from now this esteemed company is going to be putting its future in your still-soft hands, hoping I've taught you enough that you don't get ripped off in the African jungles by a wily Lebanese trader or a smiling Congolese major with a large revolver in his right hand. So let us now turn our attention to price."

"Or should I say, *prices*. As you'll recall from the sorting exercise, we have 12,000 of them. The average person who's going to be selling you a fistful of diamonds might have a vague idea of what five or six size and quality combinations should sell for, and even then their information is likely to be out of date. That's the nice thing about controlling a hair over half the global market for diamonds" – White paused and looked down at his shoes – "a decline from more than 85% a few years ago, but still not a bad showing." Another pause, then White lifted his head and made eye contact with each person in the room. "We have more information, at every level of the supply pipeline, than anyone else in the business. The next biggest producer is less than one-third our size, and they sell through us. So no one – *no one* – knows what we do." His pride was palpable.

"And gentlemen, that knowledge is power. It is money. It is the reason our esteemed chairman, Sir Clarence Weil, is the fourth richest man in England. And it is what will make you a reasonably well-off man yourself, if you just pay attention to the gems of wisdom I am imparting to you. And with that, I believe it's time for tea."

Clifford had to laugh. The fellow on his right looked shocked at the show of disrespect, but Clifford couldn't have cared less. White was a pretentious, arrogant little twit with a chip on his shoulder, but he was also amusing if you didn't take him too seriously. Plus, he seemed to know what he was talking about. And unlike the lectures he'd endured at Oxford, this one was about something he could actually use. Soon. For just two months from now, he would be handed a ticket to the Democratic Republic of Congo and a briefcase with $1 million in cash.

When that day came, Clifford found his extensive training left him completely unprepared for the first challenge he faced as a diamond buyer. He landed at N'Djili International Airport in Kinshasa tired, a bit smelly, but feeling well-pleased with himself. All his life he'd wanted to be anything but another upper-middle-class bore, one of those people who find a way to work the fact they once saw Prince Charles (from a great distance) into every conversation. And now here he was, starting an adventure most people couldn't even imagine. He felt extraordinarily cool and sophisticated, a true man of the world.

"Papers," the bored-looking Immigration Official demanded. Clifford handed him his passport.

"What's in the briefcase?"

"Confidential work material, I'm afraid."

"Open it."

"As I said, the material inside is confidential."

"I don't care what it is. Open the case."

"I'm with Delacroix. We send people through here all the time, and all of them carry a briefcase exactly like this one."

"And they all open that briefcase. Now it's your turn."

"Perhaps we could go somewhere a bit more private?"

"As you wish. Put your hands behind your back. You are under arrest."

Clifford pleaded with the man to release him. "I work for Delacroix. Call the office here. I'm sure they'll tell you everything is ok."

"They might. We'll find out tomorrow."

"Tomorrow? You mean I have to spend the night in jail?"

"Young man, you have refused a direct order from a Customs Official of the Democratic Republic of the Congo. You are suspected of smuggling, which is a very serious offense in this country. If your stay in our jail is limited to just one night, you should count yourself very lucky indeed."

15 minutes later, relieved of his passport, his luggage and – most important – his $1 million briefcase, Clifford heard the cell door clank shut. He was now sharing a space not much larger than his extended arms with eight very tough, very angry looking men. "Don't recall anything about this in the training sessions," he muttered unhappily.

One by one, the other men in the cell fell asleep. Not Clifford. Being arrested upon arrival was annoying; being raped was an entirely different matter.

At precisely 8AM an overly cheery British voice broke the stillness with "Good morning and welcome to the DRC! I trust the accommodations were to your liking?"

"Who the hell are you?" Clifford grunted.

"I am Thomas B. Milton, your man on the ground here in Kinshasa. Originally from Kent, but now An Old Africa Hand. My job is to ensure that fresh meat like yourself gets thrown in with the lambs instead of the lions."

"And your job description doesn't involve working in the evening, much less greeting new arrivals *before* they get arrested?"

"Where's the fun in that? Arrest Upon Arrival is a grand tradition in Kinshasa. Surely you wouldn't want to be deprived of your chance to join The Pantheon? 'Got to the airport and went to my hotel' doesn't have quite the same ring when you're telling stories to your mates, now does it?"

Clifford had to admit that it didn't. And the surprising thought struck him that once he got cleaned up and managed a good night's sleep, this might well be a rather satisfying badge of honor with which to begin his adventures. So he made up his mind to adopt Thomas B. Milton's approach and treat this whole thing as an excellent laugh.

"Clifford Watkins, at your service," he said.

"That much is certainly true. The service part, that is. You'll need to pay back the $500 it cost me to get you out of this place."

CHAPTER 16

The DRC

After a quick shower and breakfast, Clifford joined Milton for the drive to a smaller, military airport where one of Delacroix's fleet of small planes was waiting. "It could have been worse, you know," said Milton. "One pile of fresh meat got married the week before he came down here, and thought it was a good idea to bring his new wife along. They got to spend their honeymoon in the same deluxe accommodations you enjoyed last night."

"How did she take it?"

"Not so well. Walked out of the police station, hailed a taxi, and went straight back to London. Didn't even bother to pick up her bags. The divorce papers arrived two weeks later."

"So I'm doing well by comparison?"

"You're a star, Clifford, an absolute star. Now, your flight will take about 45 minutes. It will land in the middle of nowhere on a dirt strip so pot-holed you'll refuse to call it a runway. If you have back problems, prepare to writhe in agony. Resist the temptation to jump out of the plane: it's a good way to get your head chopped off. And even I can't help you with that one.

"Only after the propeller blades have stopped turning *completely* should you grab your elegant handbag and make your way to the exit. From that point on I assume you know what to do."

"How long have I got on the ground?"

"As long as it takes. The plane will wait."

"What happens if there's trouble?"

"You mean, what happens if someone sticks a gun in your face and demands an immediate cash withdrawal?"

"That's a good place to start."

"Then the heavily armed guards who travel with the plane start shooting. All seriousness aside, the guys you'll be trading with *look* pretty tough, and in other circumstances they probably are. But they're smart enough to know that anyone who arrives by private plane is likely to have some serious resources behind him. And while we don't put our name on our planes for security reasons, everyone in the business can spot them a mile away. There are very few bad guys who want to tango with the Cartel."

"So you're saying it's completely safe?"

"*Oh my God no, of course it's not safe*! You're holding more money that most of these guys will make in 10,000 years. Someone is likely to take a shot. My only point is that it's unlikely to be a guy in drawstring pants and no shirt. But if you see a group of guys in military green approaching with rifles at shoulder height, I strongly suggest you make your way back to your assigned seat and tell the pilot to get the hell out of there."

"Has anyone ever had a... bad experience out here?"

"About two years ago one of the planes got shot down. Everyone was ok, but the diamonds got scattered around the bush."

"What did you do?"

"Brought in our security experts. They set up a perimeter around the crash site, and removed six inches of topsoil from the entire area. It was all flown back to Jo'burg where some unfortunate had to sift through literally tons of dirt, brush and other assorted crap in order to find all the diamonds."

"Did they?"

"In that way Delacroix is a bit like the US Marines: we never leave a stone behind. So yes, they got every single diamond. Took nearly two months, but they got them."

"So to summarize, your advice is, 'Try not to be attacked by paramilitary groups'."

"That's it! If you just do that, you should be fine. What perfect timing: your chariot awaits. Goodbye, young Watkins. Try to stay alive and out of jail, won't you? I have a rather busy afternoon. The cricket is on."

Clifford smiled as he shook the man's hand, knowing that behind the veneer of carefree cynicism Thomas B. Milton was a man who could get things done in God-forsaken places. It would be wise to stay on his good side.

For nearly 45 minutes the old Embraer flew low over the jungle, finally landing on the dirt runway that was every bit as jarring as Milton had promised. The brakes slammed on, dust flew everywhere, and the young pilot turned around in his seat to look at his primary passenger. "Thank you for flying with us today on Air Nowhere!"

Clifford provided the requisite smile of appreciation, picked up the briefcase full of money, and walked down the three steps onto African soil. The pilot came around to pull out a folding table and chair that had been stowed in the tiny cargo area, and helped Clifford set them up. Two minutes later he was ready for business.

Except there wasn't any.

For more than an hour Clifford sat, feeling his confidence replaced by concern with each passing minute. Other than the pilot and two guards, there wasn't another human being in sight.

"A bit slow, wouldn't you say?" asked Clifford.

It was the larger of the guards who replied. "It's always this way when new meat comes to town. Everyone wants to sniff you a bit before they approach."

"And where might that everyone be? I can't see a soul."

"You just need to learn how to look. Men who live in the bush get good at hiding, but it's not humanly possible for them to see us without us being able to see them. It's the eyes that give them away. See that copse of trees at 2 o'clock? If you look hard enough you'll see at least seven pairs of eyes. They've been there since five minutes after the plane touched down."

"Should I approach them?"

"Only if you'd like to get shot. Most of these guys have not had good experiences with white men leading a band of armed guards in their direction."

That was sensible enough. Clifford just wished that smug Mr. White had devoted less of his training lectures to the physical properties of diamonds, and a little more to how to stay alive in the African bush.

Clifford got drawn so deeply into these thoughts he didn't see the tall but practically emaciated man standing in front of him. It was only when the man opened his hand and let three reasonably sized rough diamonds tumble onto the folding table that Clifford managed to look up. Undoubtedly the blackest man he'd ever seen. No shirt. No shoes. Too-big pants held on with a rope tied around his waist. This was where the glamorous world of diamonds began.

Clifford inspected the three stones very carefully, and wrote a number on a piece of paper. The man looked disappointed, but nodded his head in agreement. Clifford Watkins, of Seaford, Sussex, the United Kingdom, was now an African diamond trader.

CHAPTER 17

Gaborone, May 18, 6:47 p.m.

It had not been a good day for Inspector McLean. Delacroix had yet to respond to the request for access to all their Botswana operations. Perhaps Thomas had asked rather than insisted. Perhaps Delacroix had something to hide. But over the years McLean had found the most common explanation for this sort of delay is that big companies simply cannot do anything quickly – especially once the damn lawyers get involved. Figuring a change of pace might help his mood, McLean dragged himself to the hotel's casino.

The in-room brochure promised "modern, glitzy interiors" – is "glitzy" now a good thing, he wondered? – and "150 ultra modern slot machines". As he looked around the offensively colorful room, McLean wondered if the copy had been written 20 years ago. At the roulette wheel stood five very broad, very strong, very drunk Russians waving fists of cash. Two Chinese entrepreneurs were playing blackjack as the ice melted far too quickly in their untouched drinks. And against all the other vacant tables leaned tall African women – Tutsis, Zulu, Tsweana – with only one thing in common: they were all for rent.

As Inspector waved away yet another bored waiter, he looked up to see an exceptionally long pair of black legs that led all the way up to a short skirt and a white blouse opened one button too many.

"Buy me a drink?"

"Normally I'd love to, but I've had a really rough day and can't manage anything more adventurous than sitting here getting quietly drunk."

"Want to tell me about it?"

"You wouldn't understand."

"So telling me would leave you no worse off than you are right now."

The Inspector smiled, having just lost Round 1 of the eternal dance. "I flew here all the way from London to investigate a murder. And the people I'd most like to interview won't let me in the door."

"Who's that, sugar?"

"The nice folks at Delacroix."

The woman threw her head back and laughed, showing off both pearly white teeth and a surprisingly delicate neck. "Don't feel bad. No one ever gets in there. Even the employees have trouble getting past Security."

"How do you know that?"

"My brother works in the sorting house."

McLean was suddenly alert. This could be the break he needed. "Did your brother ever describe the security systems for you?"

"My, my, my. Aren't you the curious sort? How do I know you're not a criminal... or a spy?" She leaned in close, showing McLean her flawless skin. *She smells like jasmine*, he thought with guilty pleasure.

"While I'm flattered by the comparison with James Bond" – McLean had a brief flashback to Edith packing his clothes for this trip – "I'm an ordinary copper. See: no martini. No dinner jacket. Just black circles under my eyes and half a glass of a rather unpleasant beer."

"Well, Mr. Ordinary Copper, could I expect some sort of reward for cooperating with your investigation?"

"Scotland Yard is not in the habit of paying for information."

"And getting paid is not a habit for me. It's an occupation. So do we have a deal?"

McLean shook his head, realizing that he'd just lost Round 2 as well. "Deal," he said.

"Now that wasn't so hard, was it? And thank you for asking: my name is Thoko."

"Where are my manners? It's nice to meet you, Thoko. My name is... Inspector McLean."

"Inspector, huh? Was that your father's name?" Thoko smiled to show she was kidding. "Obviously I don't know all the details. My brother only talks about the bits that drive him crazy."

"Like what?"

"Well, he's been working there for five years. He knows all the guards by name, and they all know him. But unless he has his ID with him, he doesn't get in."

"I suppose the ID is needed to unlock doors once he gets inside the building."

"Could be, though you'd think they could just lend him one on those rare occasions he forgets to bring his own."

"True. But I have to say, requiring employees to bring their ID each day doesn't sound all that unreasonable."

"It's not, but I've only told you what happens on the way in. That's the easy part. After all, no one ever tries to smuggle things *in* to a diamond company."

You'd be surprised, thought McLean.

"Getting *out* is much harder. There's an X-ray inspection. They say it's low-dose radiation... but they would, wouldn't they? My brother is worried that some day he's going to get cancer, or grow an extra head, and it will be because he got zapped one time too many." The Inspector could see that despite the playful word choice, Thoko was genuinely concerned about her brother's health. "There's also a 1 in 10 chance you'll be singled out for a cavity search, and I'm not talking about teeth."

"How did they decide who gets the, um, closer inspection?"

"Supposedly it's random, but my brother says it always pays to stay on the good side of the guards."

"Does anyone ever actually try to steal diamonds?"

"All the time! The company says nothing about it publicly – for obvious reasons – but you always hear stories."

"Has anyone ever succeeded?"

"If they did, they're unlikely to talk about it. Security at Delacroix has very long arms."

"So are you saying their systems are foolproof?"

"Definitely not. Once my brother came home and found a tiny diamond had fallen into the gap between his belt and his pants."

"And no one noticed it was missing?"

"Are you kidding? They made my brother's entire team search for that diamond for four hours before they let them go home. When it fell out of his pants my brother couldn't decide if it was funny or humiliating. He said taking the stone back the next day was one of the hardest things he's ever had to do."

"But that was an accident. What about deliberate theft?"

"People try. They stick diamonds in their cheeks, or at the back of their throats. Up their noses, in their backsides – every single hole you can think of. And I mean *every* one. Some people even swallow them."

"Does that work?"

"Nah. If the guards even think that's what happened, they lock you up in a small room with nothing but a bed and a toilet. And then they check all your bowel movements until the stone comes out."

"You can't be serious."

"Honey, if you get serious with me right now, I'll introduce you to my brother when we're done."

God he was tempted. But the last time he'd been down that road it hadn't worked out very well: for him, his career, or his marriage.

What is it about black women, McLean wondered, that made him do truly stupid things? The last time she had been a goddamned material witness. In a homicide investigation. But somehow he'd convinced himself that the long dinners in bistros far from home were part of his interrogation. That the wine was to help lower her guard, and perhaps reveal new information.

Weak as that excuse was, it went flying out the window of her tiny flat in Islington the first time he spent the night there.

How was he to know she was being watched by the Vice Squad?

Not a day passed when he didn't recall that horrible feeling of sitting in the King's Arms while his old buddy Phillip laid out the 8 x 10 photos of him entering the apartment, and leaving seven hours later with a scratch on his neck and a goofy grin on his face. It had cost £1,000 for those pictures to be "lost" on their way back to the file. But even Phillip couldn't get rid of the surveillance records showing a "man, approx. 6'3" and 210 pounds" paying an overnight visit to a known prostitute.

Gaborone, May 18, 6:47 p.m.

McLean looked up at Thoko's strong cheekbones and flawless coffee-colored skin, then forced his eyes back to his drink. This time he was determined to let his brain make the decision.

CHAPTER 18

The DRC

Over time, Clifford found himself dividing his suppliers into two types. A man with no shirt was in business for himself, either scooping up the riverbed or digging holes in the mud to search below the surface. This was the most dangerous form of mining, for few diggers could afford the wood needed to reinforce the walls of their ramshackle mines, and dozens were killed every year when – after rain soaked the ground – the sides gave way and buried them underneath several feet of heavy, choking mud. It took a brave and desperate man to face these risks day in and day out, and Clifford always treated them with respect.

Less so the men in army uniforms. They were parasites. They would "stand guard" while the shirtless risked their lives, then swoop in whenever a diamond was found. Sometimes they would buy the stone, unilaterally setting the price based on their "knowledge of market conditions", which was just an eloquent way of saying "that's the price – take it or leave it". More often than not, however, they would simply commandeer the diamond, claiming the shirtless owed it to them for "license fees" or "protection services".

Clifford despised the soldiers, and took a perverse pride in showing them the same lack of respect they gave the diggers. He knew he couldn't push it too far; the soldiers were armed and many thought nothing of shooting someone who had the temerity to stand up to their mad authority. But Clifford also knew the company plane parked behind him was a reminder that he, too, had friends in powerful places.

Clifford spent nearly five years traveling back and forth to Africa, developing a reputation for both a discerning eye and excellent negotiating skills. For him it was the perfect life, half his time spent in remote locations doing a storybook job, and half spent back in London telling his beautiful friends tales than left them slack-jawed. He was undeniably cool, and even the most beautiful of the tanned blonde Princess Diana wannabe's who hung on his every word would have readily agreed to spend the night with him.

Except Clifford wasn't interested in that sort of thing. Never had been. His tastes ran to men, but they didn't run very hard. One or two a year, as much out of boredom as sexual or emotional interest. And never with anyone he might see again. Clifford was one of those rare individuals who enjoyed company far more than intimacy. And here, too, his job was a perfect fit.

But all that changed in 2000, when Delacroix made the landmark decision to sell only those diamonds they had mined themselves. As NGO's like Global Witness and Amnesty International focused worldwide attention on the issue of blood diamonds, there was a rapidly growing risk that even a handful of stones from war-torn countries like Sierra Leone, Angola and the Democratic Republic of Congo could damage the reputation of the category as a whole.

Rather than risk losing everything just to keep buying what was ultimately a small number of stones – well less than 4% of the global total – Delacroix made the difficult decision to stop buying diamonds on the open market. And that meant the end of the line for the bush traders.

Intellectually Clifford understood and even agreed with this break with history. But that didn't relieve the sorrow and rising anger he felt as he flew out of Africa for the last time. A life he had loved was now gone forever, to be replaced by precisely the sort of mindless, soulless corporate bowing and scraping he had always despised. For the company had decided that the field agents were to return to head office where they would be magically transformed into Account Executives. Each would be responsible for about eight Delacroix clients. The job description was simple: ensure those clients are happy.

It sounded easy. In practice it was a nightmare.

The single most important principle of the diamond industry is that demand almost always exceeds supply, usually by a factor of two to three times. That means clients are never, ever satisfied; Sisyphus had it easy by comparison.

Clifford hated it. He had gone from doing what he wanted when he wanted, far away from oversight of any kind, to being hounded 24/7 by clients who devoted an inordinate number of their waking hours to finding something to complain about. Most of the time he would pretend to listen sympathetically, all the while resisting the urge to make the World's Tiniest Violin gesture with his fingers. And in those rare cases the client actually had a point, it frustrated him not being able to promise anything more than sympathy and a half-hearted "I'll speak to the Sales Director".

More and more he found himself flirting with the idea of making a change. A drastic change. He wanted to get back to Africa, back to trading in diamonds. While Delacroix would no longer buy from independent suppliers, there were still a lot of people who would. In some cases they were so desperate for rough – it's very hard to remain in the diamond business if you haven't got any diamonds – they were willing to overlook any little abuses that may have occurred along the supply chain. Others were genuinely concerned about the hundreds of thousands of desperately poor diggers and their families who would starve if they were unable to sell the handful of stones they managed to hide from the soldiers. If he continued to trade with them, Clifford convinced himself, he wouldn't be doing anything wrong. On the contrary, he'd be helping people, maybe even saving lives.

Ultimately Clifford's destiny was shaped not by this ethical argument, but by a change in corporate strategy. For years Delacroix had operated mines that were well past their prime, and thus losing fairly substantial sums of money. They did so simply to keep the mines out of the hands of others, thereby ensuring they maintained a dominant share of the global market. But after a decade of slow consumer demand in the 1990's, Delacroix found itself with nearly $10 billion worth of excess diamonds sitting in the basement vaults at #42 Farringdon Road. The company tried to position this as an asset that would increase in value once consumer demand rebounded – as it had throughout history. They argued that diamonds aren't like ordinary inventory, which can spoil or become outdated. They said a better comparison would be with cash in the bank.

Stock analysts, however, were not convinced. Cash in the bank would at least draw interest. Invested in the stock market, it could bring a 10% annual return. So effectively that diamond mountain Delacroix was sitting on was costing them $1 billion a year, money the analysts felt would be better spent increasing shareholder dividends or expanding into adjacent businesses. Moreover, they said, it was crazy to buy up even more diamonds at rates where profits were impossible, simply to pump up an unsustainably high market share.

The company had to admit the analysts had a point. So for the first time in its history, Delacroix put some of its mines on the market.

The response was lackluster at best. Most of the majors figured that if Delacroix couldn't make money from these mines, they couldn't either. Some smaller companies were interested, thinking that with their lower cost bases they might be able to eke out a profit. But most of them struggled to find the funding needed for the acquisition. Clifford, of course, had no money at all – other than his monthly paycheck. But he was convinced that if he could ever find a backer, owning a mine could make him rich.

In his opinion, the difficult part of diamond mining was finding the mines in the first place. Getting the diamonds out of the ground wasn't hugely different than mining for gold, platinum or other metals. And thanks to the economic downturn there was no shortage of people with the skills he needed, on the market and eager to move into something as sexy as diamonds. He would simply outsource the actual mining to people who knew what they were doing.

Clifford had also spent enough time in Delacroix's African operations to know there were a lot of costs that could be taken out. Delacroix was charged more for anything and everything than an ordinary company would be. Most Africans saw them as an obscenely rich company who had gotten that way at the expense of the locals; now it was time for them to return some of that wealth via inflated prices charged to them for everything from catering to truck tires. The Africans also expected Delacroix to make significant contributions to local charities and provide its workers with far more benefits – including free housing and medical care – than ordinary companies did. Unions demanded double-digit wage increases each year and threatened to strike if their demands were not met, highlighting the fact 1,000 workers could be paid with the chairman's salary alone.

Life for Clifford would be much easier. A halfway decent PR firm should be able to position his acquisition of a mine as "rescuing African jobs" that had been eliminated by Big Bad Delacroix. That would buy him a few years' worth of protection from complaints about the lower pay and reduced benefits he planned to offer his workers. Since it would be several years before the company made a profit – a fact he'd make sure all the press knew – no one could expect him to match Delacroix's generosity to local schools and charities. And because he had no baggage from the days of apartheid, there was little risk of radical groups like the ANC's Youth Wing singling him out in their public protests. With costs just a fraction of Delacroix's, and a free ride for at least 3-4 years on the public relations front, every piece of the puzzle was in place to do what Clifford wanted to do.

Except for the money to get it all started.

CHAPTER 19

Gaborone, March 19, 8:27 a.m.

It was Day 3 of his Big African Adventure. Inspector McLean sat in his room, chewing a thumbnail and cursing his lack of progress. It had been almost 24 hours since he made his request, and Delacroix still hadn't responded – let alone given him entrée to their local operations. The police were cordial but unhelpful. The only real information he'd gotten came from a hooker at the casino – a lovely hooker, but a hooker nonetheless - but since it was about security systems in Botswana rather than London it was unlikely to have any bearing on the case. Maybe he was wasting his time here.

Or maybe he just wasn't shaking the tree hard enough.

McLean's mind had just wandered towards chainsaws when the phone rang.

"Is this Inspector McLean of the London Metropolitan Police?"

"Yes it is. May I ask who's speaking please?"

"This is Detective TH Mabusla of the Botswana Police. I have a situation here that I thought might be of relevance to you."

"Forgive me, Detective, but where exactly is 'here'?"

"The closest town is Pontdrift, on the border with South Africa. It's about a five-hour drive from where you are now, sir."

"Detective, I'm always eager to help a fellow member of law enforcement. But that's quite a long way away, and I've got a case of my own to look after."

"I believe my case may be somehow connected with yours."

"And what makes you think that?"

"Well, we won't be able to say with any certainty until the corpse has been formally identified. But I believe the victim is Sammy Moeng, the former managing director of the Botswana office of Delacroix Mining."

McLean sat bolt upright in the cramped desk chair. "That does indeed interest me. How sure are you that's who you've got?"

"Not very, Inspector. The vultures got to the body several hours before we did, and most of the face is gone. We'll need dental records for a positive ID."

"If there's no face, what makes you think it's the ex-MD?"

"As I said, sir, I'm not sure it's him. But his wife reported him missing three days ago. What's left of the clothes matches what he was wearing the last time she saw him. And the height is the same."

"Any sign of foul play?"

"I haven't been to the crime scene yet, but the report I was given says any evidence is likely to have been moved or altered by the animals that have come to feed on the body."

McLean felt his breakfast churning in his stomach. "Fortunately we don't see a lot of that in London. And while I'm not eager to start, it sounds like the only way we're going to learn more is to go to the crime scene. How can I get there?"

"Go down to the hotel entrance in about 15 minutes. I'll have a car sent around to pick you up."

When the time came McLean noted with considerable relief that for once he wasn't going to have to squeeze in an ancient Toyota; today he would be chauffeured around in a Range Rover Discovery. Had he known Botswana a bit better, he would have realized the reason for the upgrade the moment he saw the vehicle. 30 minutes outside of Gaborone, the quality of the roads deteriorated sharply. As they approached the Tuli Block, asphalt turned to gravel. And at almost the same instant the driver said "we'll be there in 45 minutes", the roads disappeared entirely. Even holding on to the roof of the Discovery, McLean got bounced around like popcorn in a microwave oven. Every time his hips came crashing down on the well-worn seat, his liver and one of his kidneys swapped places. "I can't believe anyone goes off-road driving for *fun*," McLean muttered under his breath.

At long last the Discovery came to a halt beneath the shade of a baobab tree. A little worried about whether his legs were up to it, McLean stepped gingerly out of the car to be greeted by a very handsome man in his late 20's who immediately held out his hand. "Detective TH Mabusla at your service, Inspector. I can't thank you enough for coming."

Truer words were never uttered, McLean grumbled as he massaged his battered lower back.

TH pointed into the distance, where McLean could see a group of birds standing in a circle. Suddenly, a shot rang out. McLean instinctively reached for his gun, only to realize it was still at home on the top shelf of his bedroom closet. "I hope I didn't startle you, Inspector. I'm just trying to get rid of the vultures."

Vultures? Seriously? Maybe the mean streets of London aren't so bad after all.

The two men approached the body, while the vultures circled angrily overhead. McLean had seen a lot of death in his 23-year career, but this one nearly made him wretch. Almost all of the man's face had been torn off -- presumably by wild animals -- and the vultures had gnawed huge chunks out of the soft areas beneath the ribs and around the thighs. Both men covered their noses and mouths with their handkerchiefs, and gingerly approached what remained of the body.

"See the claw marks here on the chest? Those are from a lion."

"So you think he died from natural causes?"

"No, I'm pretty sure he didn't. If you look behind his left ear, you'll see what looks like a bullet hole. Since the skin is missing I can't say how recent it is, but you'd have to be both extremely tough and extremely lucky to survive something like that."

It took every ounce of nerve McLean had to lean closer for a better look. But when he did, the gunshot wound was clear. "Murder or suicide, detective?"

"For now I'm thinking murder. It's difficult – not impossible, but difficult – to shoot yourself behind the ear. And why bother? The temple or the throat is an easier way to go."

"That's the way I see it as well. Any idea who would have wanted him dead?"

"Assuming it wasn't a hunting accident or something like that? Probably a lot of people."

"Why do you say that?"

"Moeng helped set up Delacroix Mining – the joint venture between Delacroix and the Botswana government -- back in 1968. When he retired 27 years later, the company had revenues of almost $5 billion a year and Sammy was by far the richest man in Botswana."

"Is that a problem?"

"Tremendous wealth always produces tremendous jealousy. And at times it seemed as if Sammy went out of his way to flash his wealth in everyone's face. He bought the first Ferrari ever imported to Botswana – in fire engine red, no less. When people started complaining about someone who is arguably a public servant living that well, he didn't apologize. Instead he bought a second Ferrari."

"I can't imagine anyone taking a Ferrari on the roads I travelled this morning."

"Precisely, Inspector. He didn't buy those cars because he likes to drive fast. He bought them because he wanted to make a statement, the sort of in-your-face gesture that ordinary Batswana cannot stand."

"So is it possible someone killed him out of envy?"

"Possible, though not likely."

"What makes you say that?"

"I can't remember exactly when he bought his first Ferrari, but it was at least 10 years ago. If someone wanted to kill him for that, why wait?"

McLean had to agree that made sense. "So has anything happened recently that might have led to the mess we see before us?"

Mabusla smiled briefly, and then looked McLean in the eye. "This is going to take a while. Why don't we discuss it on the ride back to Gaborone."

CHAPTER 20

Gaborone, March 19, 5:20 p.m.

"Inspector, in this country we say 'If Delacroix didn't exist, we would have had to invent it." We have our differences with the company, and there have been some very difficult times. But it's no exaggeration to say that without the money diamonds have brought us, Botswana would probably be another backward African nation struggling to survive. Developed nations talk about 'the resource curse', but when you're as poor as we were a curse seems a small price to pay. Diamond money paid for roads, and schools, and free retroviral treatment for the many Batswana with HIV/AIDS. It pays for every child in the country to get a free education up to the age of 13. It gives us the funds to invest in building our tourism industry, and expanding mining beyond diamonds to precious metals.

"It goes without saying we owe a lot of that to Delacroix. If they hadn't discovered diamonds here, there would have been no money to pay for any of this. And they must be given credit for the 50/50 joint venture with government, that same joint venture which was once headed by the man whose body now lies in a zippered bag in the back of our truck. If you look at what's happening with the oil industry in Nigeria, or how the Chinese are exploiting naïve countries like Zimbabwe, it's clear we're lucky to have Delacroix."

"But..." McLean began.

"But it often feels like Delacroix wants *all* the credit, leaving none for Botswana. Would they have been so successful if Botswana didn't believe in transparency and the rule of law? Or if we'd nationalized the diamond fields, like Angola once did and Zimbabwe is threatening to do today? How come Delacroix doesn't have 50/50 joint ventures with South Africa or Liberia? The way we Batswana hear the story, it was our government that demanded the Equal Partners model. And while the revenue from Delacroix diamonds has flown into the coffers of South Africa, Namibia, Tanzania, Angola and other southern African countries, none of them has done with their opportunity what we have with ours. Yet you won't read about that in the Delacroix annual report."

"So the company is resented?"

"Without question. But what I've described so far is more of a love/hate thing. Things get much murkier when it comes to politics. The BDP – the Botswana Democratic Party – has been in power since the first day we became a nation. Given the tremendous growth we've seen over the last 40-plus years, that's probably not surprising. People are genuinely thankful for the progress their politicians have delivered."

"But sometimes, just to be sure, politicians like to stack the deck," McLean offered.

"Exactly, Inspector. Now bear in mind I have absolutely no proof of what we're about to discuss. But ultimately the truth isn't as important as what Sammy Moeng's murderer might have *thought*."

"And you're betting he thought Sammy diverted at least some of those diamond revenues to helping the ruling party stay in power."

"Yup. And do you know why I think that?"

"I can't wait to find out."

"Because that's what Sammy told the newspapers."

"*What?* He admitted paying bribes to government officials?"

"He didn't admit anything. He volunteered it. Actually called a press conference to announce it."

"This keeps getting better and better. Why would he do that?"

"The government had challenged his purchase of a large tract of land next to his family estate. He wanted them to back off."

"So be blackmailed them? Publicly?" McLean felt like a kid struggling to put together a jigsaw puzzle while an older sibling hid a few key pieces behind her back.

"Yes. Of course, he said he wasn't linking the two things. Claimed that he'd started feeling bad about what he'd done Back In The Day, and wanted to come clean."

"What did the government say?"

"That they had no idea what he was talking about."

"What did Delacroix say?"

"Ah, now *that* was interesting. Their official response was to categorically deny that *Delacroix* had made or facilitated any illegal payments. As for any questionable activities at the joint venture, the press would need to speak to the management of the company at the time of the supposed violation."

"Meaning Sammy himself."

"Meaning Sammy himself. Clever, isn't it?"

"Fiendishly so. How did he react?"

"He sent a statement to the *Botswana Gazette* saying he was currently in the process of organizing his notes on – let me see if I can remember the words – 'matters of interest to the nation', and would call a press conference within the next few weeks. That was two days before his wife reported him missing."

"To recap," said McLean, "we've now narrowed down the list of suspects to everyone in government, and everyone not in government."

"If you want to limit yourself to Botswana's borders, yes."

"Meaning there were people in other countries who wanted him dead as well?"

"Inspector, all of our neighbors are headed by men who are heroes of the liberation movement. Jacob Zuma in South Africa was arrested for conspiring to overthrow the Apartheid government, and sentenced to 10 years on Robben Island... where he met Nelson Mandela. Zimbabwe's Robert

Mugabe spent a decade as a political prisoner; as soon as he got out he went to rebel base camps in Mozambique to lead the war against the white Rhodesian government. In Namibia, former president Sam Nujoma was the first leader of SWAPO, who fought Apartheid South Africa for independence. These men share a special bond, and will do whatever it takes to protect one another – especially if any of the former imperial powers are involved."

"Which is why they let people like Mugabe get away with – quite literally – murder?"

"I think Mugabe is under more pressure than you realize. But it's all being done behind closed doors, so no one loses face."

"So are you saying that perhaps one of your neighbors had Moeng killed in order to spare the president of Botswana from a possibly embarrassing revelation about the past?"

"I'm saying it's unlikely to be a coincidence we found his body less than 30 miles from the border crossing with South Africa."

CHAPTER 21

Antwerp, January 26, 11:50 p.m.

Shmuel Moskowitz rarely said anything about women. Like all Orthodox Jews, he always stayed as far away from them as possible in an often-futile attempt to avoid temptation. On those rare occasions he had no choice, he absolutely refused to touch them – even to shake hands – for fear they might be "impure". So Daniel was more than a bit surprised when – during the second week of his apprenticeship – Moskowitz looked to the ladies for a metaphor about diamonds.

"Young man, if you learn just one thing from me, make sure it is this: a diamond is like a beautiful woman. You can woo her. Whisper sweet nothings in her ear. Caress her gently. Plead with her. But unless you *understand* her she will never give herself up to you."

Once he recovered from the shock of learning even Moskowitz had a romantic side, eager-to-please 16-year-old Daniel had readily agreed and promised to remember those words of wisdom forever. But it was only now, after more than 20 years in the business, that he actually understood what his mentor was trying to tell him. Because for the very first time he was faced with a diamond he was not sure would yield to his charms.

In fact, the 138-carater terrified him. With smaller diamonds Daniel could quickly spot both the potential and the pitfalls. But this diamond was just so much bigger than anything he'd ever worked with that he couldn't see through it. Its heart was a total mystery to him, and while cutting a window had marginally improved visibility, it didn't relieve the fear there was something unexpected in the center of the stone that would result in disaster.

A very expensive disaster.

Diamond prices go up exponentially with size, magnifying the importance of each cut, each pass on the polishing wheel. Lose a carat on a two-carat diamond, and you're out about $10,000. Drop that same carat on a 10-carat stone, and the loss would be closer to $100,000. That makes it important to understand the rough diamond completely, intimately, before the cutting process begins. It is such an intensely private and personal process that when the diamond is finally taken away to be sold, many cutters are reduced to tears – as if they'd lost a wife or a daughter.

Daniel knew all that, but until this morning it was a story told in the third person. Today it became real.

He thought back to his early days in the business, cutting diamonds so small it was hard for the untrained eye to be sure they even existed. The 1-2 caraters in which he now specialized were a hundred times bigger than that; surely the rough diamond sitting in front of him was just another rung on the same ladder he'd been climbing all his life?

Maybe. But the rationalization didn't make him feel one bit better. Especially when a little voice in the back of his head reminded him that this diamond had survived for 3 billion years or so, and that it would be a real shame if it died over the next few days on Daniel Stern's crowded work bench.

"Damn it," Daniel muttered, and held the stone up to his right eye. "Please, please talk to me."

It was nearly 2 AM when Daniel finally lay down in bed, praying that exhaustion would bring the sleep he so badly needed. It had been a frustrating day. He wasn't expecting to accomplish much the first time out, but as he stared at the ceiling he realized he had hoped for some sort of inspiration – even a faint glimmer of light that would illuminate the path he needed to take. No such luck. There were moments in the late afternoon when he found himself hating the 138-carater, angry at its total and inscrutable silence.

If there was only someone he could talk to, someone who could give him advice on how to get started. But Daniel had shut the door on that option the second he purchased an exceptional diamond from a total stranger for a truly ridiculous price. Although he still wasn't sure what was wrong with it, he was certain the diamond was less than completely clean. And while people in the industry had been known to overlook a bit of questionable dealing in search of greater profits, you had to be very careful about who you brought into your confidence. Choose wrongly, and Daniel could find himself thrown out of the industry altogether. He might even land in jail. No, Daniel had made his bed and now he had to lie in it.

Then a thought struck Daniel like a punch in the gut: he missed Moskowitz. The old man with the breath that smelled like chopped liver. His huge belly engulfing Daniel's shoulder every time he peered down at what the young apprentice was doing on the polishing wheel. And that look of soul-crushing disappointment he wore whenever Daniel brought him a half-completed diamond for inspection.

The old bastard had treated him like a servant incapable of doing anything right. It had taken more than 6 months for Daniel to graduate from boart – cheap, small, nearly worthless diamonds used mostly for training purposes – to commercial goods. And each step up took Daniel far longer than any of the other apprentices.

After five years of constant rejection, Daniel could take no more. When he handed in his resignation, Moskowitz looked more disappointed than angry. "Someday, God willing, I hope you learn." Daniel had reddened at the insult, and stormed out of the workshop determined to humiliate the old man. He had been reasonably successful at his next employer, and done well enough to set up his own, admittedly small business before he was 30. But the shame of Moskowitz's rejection had never left him.

And now he realized the man he hated more than anyone in the world was right: he *didn't* get it.

He'd never learned how to persuade "the beautiful woman" to share her secrets. Instead, he'd learned to dress her up well enough that she could pass muster in polite society. And that was good enough with ordinary diamonds. But for the first time in his life he had come face to face with one so beautiful it made your heart stop, and he couldn't think of a thing to say to her. He had technique, but no soul. He was not, in the words of old Moskowitz, a true *diamantaire*.

Helluva time for that little epiphany, Daniel thought angrily as he got out of bed to pour himself yet another drink.

CHAPTER 22

Gaborone, March 19, 9:20 p.m.

The shebeen was small and shabby, really just a shack with a corrugated steel roof. The bar counter – such as it was – was an old plank resting on two barrels. The walls were patched together from scraps of wood. There were a few chairs and two highly coveted tables near the back. But despite its impoverished condition, the shebeen was always packed. And tonight was no exception.

TH quickly spotted his friend Kitso, squeezed his way through the tightly packed crowd, and collapsed onto the chair Kitso had been saving for him at great personal risk.

"Do you think he bought it?"

"Hard to say. He doesn't talk much. Asks a lot of questions but doesn't offer opinions."

"That's unusual... for a Brit."

"I know. And I think it could be a problem for us."

"How so?"

"Because even if he buys our story, he's unlikely to share it with anyone else. And that defeats the whole purpose."

Kitso passed the paint bucket filled with a cheap homemade beer made from maize. "Got a better idea?"

"I might. Maybe we've been going about this all wrong. Maybe we shouldn't be using a policeman at all."

"But you said people would believe it if a policeman said it."

"And that's true. But McLean is no fool. He gives away just enough to get you to answer his questions, but not one iota more. He's not going to speculate publicly about an open case, especially one that may have nothing to do with the case he's working on."

His friend cracked his knuckles so loudly they could be heard over the din. "Say you're right. What's our next move?"

"The press."

"TH, we talked about that. You know if you let something slip the papers will report it as having come from 'police sources who must remain confidential'. And it will take your boss the better part of 10 seconds to figure out that the person most likely to have been running his mouth about your case… is you."

"That's if we're dealing with the local press. Let's face it: everyone knows our newspapers print what officials want them to. And so no one believes what they read. But they still believe what they *hear*, especially when it's gossip that supposedly comes from a reputable source that just happens to be so far away no one can ever check for accuracy."

Kitso was silent for a bit, then drained the remnants of the beer. "I understand the theory. But how are you going to make it work?"

"Moeng ran Delacroix Mining, right? That means diamonds, and diamonds are a secretive industry. Delacroix almost never talks, and when they do it's through a press release that has lots of words but says absolutely nothing. The Russians know better than to say anything publicly that isn't a quote from Dostoevsky or Gogol. And no one cares what the Aussies have to say unless it's about sport."

"Yeah, so?"

"Well, nature abhors a vacuum. If the people who know ain't talking, the people who don't know start gossiping. We just need to give them a little nudge."

"I'm getting the feeling you may have a few thoughts on that."

TH ordered a beer, and continued. "Yup. Tomorrow night you and I are going to have a few drinks at that fancy new place next to the Diamond Industrial Park. Odds are it will be crawling with people who work in the compound. We make sure they happen to overhear our conversation about who might have killed Moeng. The next day everyone will be talking about it around the water cooler. And eventually it will reach the ears of somebody who knows somebody at one of the trade publications."

"What makes you think they'll publish an unsubstantiated rumor overheard in a bar?"

"Those guys are so desperate for stuff to fill their pages they'll print anything."

"Maybe, but will anyone see it?"

"We only need one. Because then he'll ask his friend whether *he's* seen it, and an hour later everyone will be talking as if it were fact reported in a reputable newspaper, not some bullshit that you and I made up."

"Could it be traced back to us?"

"Worst case scenario, somebody says they heard us discussing it in the bar. We say we were just chatting about a rumor we'd heard earlier in the day. No one will be able to prove it was us who started the whole thing. And even if we did, the worst we can be accused of is carelessness. That's a helluva lot easier to survive than a press leak."

"Are you going to tell the boss what you're up to?"

"Nah. He told me to 'handle it' in that tone of voice he uses when he means 'but don't you dare tell me how you do it'."

"Explain to me again why our lords and masters make so much more money than we do," Kitso said as he finished off his beer.

Two days later the story was front-page news in *Diamond Insider*:

```
FOUL PLAY SUSPECTED IN DEATH OF FORMER MD OF
              DELACROIX MINING

    Suspicion Focuses on Neighbor To The South
```

Gaborone, March 19, 9:20 p.m.

Three days ago the on-line edition of this paper reported that Sammy Moeng, Managing Director of Delacroix Mining from 1968 to 1995, had been found dead in the Tuli Block near Botswana's border with South Africa. At that time police were unsure as to the cause of death, as the body had been so badly mauled by wild animals that forensic work was nearly impossible. However an initial report released by the Coroner's Office on Monday revealed there is a bullet hole in Moeng's skull, behind the left ear. In response to questioning, police were careful to emphasize they don't know if the wound was pre- or post-mortem, and therefore cannot say if it was the cause of death. They also refused to comment on whether they are treating the case as murder or suicide.

However *Diamond Insider*'s confidential sources say the focus of the investigation has shifted to a band of white mercenaries operating out of South Africa. Little is known about the group, which some have suggested has ties to the UK. But it is widely believed to have done "wet" work for governments in southern Africa looking to keep their own hands clean.

Given Moeng's recent allegations of official government corruption in Botswana, it's likely there are many people who are happy to see him dead. Whether they had any involvement in his apparent murder will only be known in time.

Government press offices in both South Africa and Botswana were unavailable for comment when this issue of *Diamond Insider* went to press.

CHAPTER 23

Johannesburg, January 7, noon

"Charles, this is Clifford. I think we may have a small problem."

"Go on."

"A man came to see me today. A very large Afrikaner with blonde hair and a nasty-looking scar."

"It's your lucky day, Clifford!"

"He was not my type at all. Especially after he pulled out his gun."

"I'm assuming that's not a euphemism."

"No, it's not. This is serious, Charles. Could you at least try to pay attention?"

"Sorry. Go ahead."

"He said his name was Frans. Didn't give a last name. Started by trying to intimidate me, you know, by leaning over my desk with his fists on the desk blotter like a gorilla, getting so close I had no choice but to pull back. Then he accused me of seeding the mine."

"What did you say?"

"I told him I had no idea what he was talking about. And then I gave him the crusher story."

"Did he buy it?"

"Of course not. He may be big, but he's not dumb."

"Did he say who he's working for?"

"No, just that his boss had taken up a lot of shares in the IPO, and wasn't pleased with our performance since then."

"Understandable. Did you explain that whether or not you find *any* diamonds – much less a big one – is very much a matter of luck?"

"Of course! I'm not an idiot. But as I said, neither is he."

There was a long pause, as Charles gave Clifford time to calm down. "Clifford, I'm sure having an armed man in your office has upset you. But the worst thing to do now is panic. We have a good plan, and we've executed it reasonably well. People may wonder how we could find so many large diamonds in a mine Delacroix said was tapped out. The more cynical may even suspect there's something going on. But that's all it is: suspicion."

"All true, Charles, but this guy *knows*."

"Clifford, there are only two people on this earth who know what we've done, and they're both on this call. Frank or Frans or whatever his name is was just trying to shake the tree to see if anything would fall out. Don't let him rattle you."

"I'll keep it together. You don't need to worry about that. But do you think maybe we should up the number of large stones we find – at least for the next six months or so? That should calm everyone down, and support our contention that in this business it's all cyclical."

Charles silently counted to ten. "You know, Clifford, that's an excellent idea. We'll do exactly as you suggest. I'm not sure how many large stones we have left in inventory, but I'll see if I can find something appropriate for you."

"Thanks, but please do it quickly. The sooner I can announce a major new piece of rough the sooner I can stop thinking about that overgrown bully."

"Understood, Clifford. I'll get on it right away. And thanks for bringing this to my attention so quickly; I feel good about where we've come out."

"Me, too. Thank you Charles."

"Goodbye, Clifford." Lithwick hung up the phone, and smiled.

"You played that perfectly, boss."

"Thank you, Frans. You did equally well, I must say."

"Yeah, but I didn't appreciate that "overgrown" comment.

"You'd prefer – what – "massively muscled"?

"Badass sonovabitch works for me."

Charles gave a little laugh. "You may get the chance to tell Clifford yourself, sooner rather than later. I wouldn't describe him as a liability – at least, not yet. But he's clearly a loose cannon that needs to be tied down. And we need to pick up the pace on our backup plan."

"Daniel Stern said he'll finish the 138-carater by a week from Tuesday."

"Do you believe him?"

"I don't know anything about cutting diamonds. But I do know when a man is out of his depth, and Stern is about a mile under water."

"Well, fear is an excellent motivator. Check in with him every few days, and make vague references to 'very important people' who are 'concerned that the diamond be completed on time'."

"Can do, boss."

"Don't mention this to Daniel now, as we don't want fear turning to panic. But if he does a tolerable job with this stone, we'll be sending more work his way."

"Another huge one?"

"I think not. The next large one our nervous Mr. Watkins finds will probably have to go through more public channels. But an ongoing relationship with Daniel is our best insurance against him deciding to come clean. What's his core business again?"

"1 -2 caraters."

"Ok. See that he gets 50-100 of those. That should keep him busy for a while."

"What about Clifford? Did you mean what you said about running short of large stones?"

"Of course not. I've got enough in the safe to keep both Clifford and Daniel busy for the next 10 years, and new stones coming in all the time. I thought for a while that Angola and maybe the DRC were going to move out of the shadows, but fortunately there are a lot of people in high places who prefer to deal directly with us, rather than those messy official channels that never seem get money into the right hands. I see nothing but great things ahead for us, Frans, and if they're smart Clifford and Daniel will come along for the ride."

"I love watching you work, boss."

"Coming from you, Frans, that's high praise indeed."

CHAPTER 24

Gaborone, Three Years Earlier

Clifford had thought about that night a hundred times, usually while lying awake at three in the morning examining the strange path his life had taken ever since. Many of the details were so clear it was like watching them on DVD. But his memory got a bit fuzzier when it came to the single most important twist in the tale.

Blame it on the booze.

The sequence of events that nearly destroyed Clifford began a very long time ago. For decades Delacroix had prided itself on being one big happy family. While the company didn't pay particularly well, it did offer a long list of benefits unlikely to be found anywhere else – at least since the Victorian Era. New employees spent part of their first day with the company tailor. Those in head office were given tasteful wool suits, while those who would be working with diamonds got uniforms without pockets (where diamonds could be hidden). Each office had a company restaurant – never ever to be called a mere "canteen" – serving breakfast, lunch, dinner and snacks throughout the day. In recent years fully equipped gyms were added. For Christmas every employee received a turkey from the Weil family farm, even though it wasn't the easiest thing to carry home on the underground. Employees wanting to buy a house could get a low-interest loan from the company. Need a car? The company would buy it for you and offer an interest-free repayment scheme.

Add a very lucrative pension scheme and the excitement of working with diamonds, and turnover was extremely low. That lulled management into thinking their employees were both happy and professionally fulfilled. The bosses were so confident, in fact, that when a research agency invited them to be part of a global employee satisfaction survey they eagerly signed up, certain they would come out at the top of the pack.

Instead they were crushed.

The numbers were bad enough, but the qualitative feedback was scathing. Employees found the gifts more patronizing than pleasing, and said they'd prefer reduced benefits and higher salaries. They felt management didn't respect or even listen to their opinions. Several said the company had more in common with the military than a successful multinational. There were concerns about not having enough Affirmative Action, offset by concerns about having too much. Employees in joint ventures said they felt like kids torn between two parents on the verge of divorce; "it's like every time I come home from school Mom wants to tell me what a horrible man my father is", said one.

Management couldn't believe it. The chairman said "I feel like a foolish old man who hasn't noticed his children have grown up and now have minds of their own." To its credit, the Executive Committee didn't try to solve the problem itself. Instead its members scheduled the first-ever Global Management Conference, which the committee called "Future Vision". And they chose to hold it in Botswana rather than London as a symbolic return to the company's African roots. Nearly 250 people were "invited", representing every aspect of the company from mining to marketing.

Unfortunately, old habits die hard. Instead of simply saying "tell us what's on your minds", the company felt obligated to "make good use of people's precious time" by scheduling every minute of the three-day event. Most of the sessions were PowerPoint presentations by the various division heads, who were under orders to be positive and uplifting.

A disinterested observer of the first morning would have noticed that each time a speaker mentioned "Mission Statement" or "End State Vision", most of the eyebrows in the room went up in an expression torn between boredom and disgust. But it takes a brave executive to wander off script when that script has been dictated from On High. In fact, it wasn't until Day Two that someone had the courage to turn off the projector. And much to everyone's surprise, it was the CFO.

"Instead of taking you through the presentation I've prepared, I'll just circulate a copy of the charts later today. Please have a look at them and let me know if you have any questions. For the next hour, I'd like to open the floor to a discussion of the results of the Employee Satisfaction Survey. Over to you."

Silence.

"With this spotlight in my eyes it's a bit hard to see you out there in the audience, but I'm going to assume at least a few of you are still awake." Modest, uncertain laughter. "Let me get the ball rolling. I'm honored to work for such a famous company. I am truly passionate about our product. I think we do some things very, very well. And when it comes to the mining and marketing of diamonds no one else comes close. But there are times I feel like I'm back in school, with Teacher telling me when I can speak, how to dress, and even what to eat for lunch. There are days that really pisses me off."

The room exploded. Hands shot up. People fought for the microphone, each more eager than the last to say something that had been bottled up inside for years. Two hours later they were still going strong, and the CFO's suggestion of a break went unheeded. Top management had hoped that a lunch recess would allow them to draw a line under the mutiny, but the Head of HR suggested food be brought in instead. It wasn't until 6 PM that the venting had exhausted itself sufficiently for the MD to call it a day. Private conversations continued at a healthy clip while people pulled together their notebooks and pre-reading packs, and slowly made their way back to their rooms to get ready for dinner. It was close to 7 p.m. before top management were able to find a quiet corner to discuss the train wreck.

"Well. That was not what I was expecting from today's agenda," the MD said angrily, slamming shut his notebook for emphasis.

Gaborone, Three Years Earlier

The CFO knew the barb was aimed at him. "Look. You can fire me if you want, but I said what I thought needed to be said. The research showed we've got a problem, and unless we let our senior managers talk about why that is and what we can do about it, we're going to get equally bad results next year. Plus there's the opportunity cost of having a staff that is less than 100% committed and inspired. For *financial* reasons alone, this is some surgery we have no choice but to undergo."

The chairman spoke up. "Don't be silly. No one is going to get fired. Quite the contrary. It takes guts to do what you did, though next time you might want to warn someone ahead of time."

"Point taken, sir."

"I feel rather like a punching bag that's had all the stuffing knocked out of it. I suspect we all need some time to catch our breath, and absorb what we saw today. Can I therefore suggest we leave it where it is for now, have a nice dinner with our colleagues – and perhaps a medicinal drink or two in the bar afterwards – and then meet at 6 AM in the breakfast room to agree how we play Day 3?"

The suggestion was met with nodded heads and sighs of relief all around.

Clifford had been eavesdropping from what he hoped was an unobtrusive spot just outside the elevators. He'd been hoping for a bit more finger-pointing and perhaps a dollop of drama, so the uneventful conclusion to the meeting came as a disappointment. He was just about to make his escape when he saw the chairman headed towards the elevator – alone. In all the years he'd worked for Delacroix, he'd never had a chance to speak to its legendary leader, much less have a private conversation. Seizing his chance, he jumped into the elevator just as the doors were closing.

Clarence Weil didn't even look up.

"That was more exciting than the usual parade of PowerPoint presentations," Clifford offered.

Weil raised one eyebrow, and sighed. "Perhaps more excitement than one should have in a single day."

"I really don't know how you do it, sir. With more than 25,000 people in the company – each of whom wants something different – it simply isn't possible to make everyone happy all of the time."

"No, of course not. But it appears we need to do a better job making some of the people happy some of the time."

"I would have thought that's the responsibility of us senior managers. Top management should be focused on the things that will make a difference to the future of this company, like strategy, government relations, and leveraging the Delacroix brand into areas beyond mining."

For the first time Clarence actually looked at the person speaking to him. "Well, I certainly feel that way. Or perhaps I should be using the past tense. There are limits to what one can do, but ultimately if there's a problem that impacts company performance, it's *my* problem."

By this point the elevator had reached the top floor, and both men took a few steps to clear the doors. "If I may ask, sir, with so many demands on your time, how do you go about deciding what to focus on?"

Clarence laughed. "Usually the decision isn't mine to make. Most days I feel like a fireman in the middle of a hot dry summer." Clarence put his right hand in his pocket, and looked at his watch – clearly buying time to think about something. "Listen: I have a few calls to make, but why don't we sit together at dinner tonight? I could use a sympathetic ear... and perhaps even a drink or three."

"I would be honored, sir." As the chairman turned to go to his suite, Clifford allowed himself a small smile. He had been right: despite the crowd of people who followed Clarence Weil wherever he went, he was actually a very lonely man. Perhaps even shy. Because of his position he spent his entire life choosing his words very, very carefully. And like everyone else he occasionally needed the release that comes from talking about trivial matters with someone completely unimportant. Clifford was more than happy to play that role; after all, it always pays to have friends in the highest places.

The two men reconnected during cocktails, and walked together into the Grand Palm Hotel's massive ballroom. After the wine was served, Clifford turned to Clarence and asked "Did you ever consider not following your father into the family business, maybe becoming a professor or a diving instructor instead of running Delacroix?" At first Weil looked surprised by the question, but quickly the look of puzzlement was replaced by sheer pleasure. It had been a while since he'd had a chat about something that wasn't materially relevant to the company's share price.

From there the conversation went to schools, and Clarence learned he and Clifford were both Oxford men. That led to reminiscing about favorite pubs, lazy spring afternoons punting down the Isis, the truly horrendous food at New College, and the magnificent meal had once a year when Magdalen College culled the deer herd that roamed their extensive grounds.

The men continued chatting amiably as the dessert plates were cleared away, and most people retired either to the bar or to bed. But Clifford and Clarence carried on, pouring wine for one another like Japanese businessmen, and ignoring the banqueting staff who were hinting a bit too broadly that the dinner was long since over. At one point Clarence interlaced his fingers and stretched out, an action that caused him to notice his watch for the first time in hours. "Goodness! Is that the time?"

"Sorry, sir. I got so caught up in what you were saying I completely lost track."

"Not at all. In fact, I'm rather keen to hear how your attempt to sabotage the fox hunt went, but I have a 11 PM call booked with the lawyers in Luxembourg. I tell you what: if you don't mind being bored for a bit, come on up with me and as soon as I finish we'll see what damage we can do to the mini bar in my suite."

Gaborone, Three Years Earlier

Encouraged by the chairman, Clifford didn't wait for the call to end before commencing his assault on the in-room fridge. He was on his fourth vodka by the time Clarence hung up, and that was on top of the nearly three bottles of wine they had polished off over dinner.

Plus the champagne for the toast. Did I have a second glass? Would have been churlish not to. Oh, my. I seem to be well and truly drunk. "I must apologize, Mr. Chairman. I seem to have indulged rather extravagantly at your expense."

"After a day like today I think a man deserves a drink. What have you been imbibing? Vodka? Time for a man's drink: Scotch all around."

And so it went. For as long as Clifford could remember.

It was nearly 5:30 when the bright African sun forced him to open his eyes. At first he couldn't figure out where he was, only that his head felt like someone was pounding it with a brick. He tried to sit up, but failed. However the effort did provide him with an important piece of information about his whereabouts: he was on the living room sofa. Not the bed. That's good. Next, check for clothes. Shirt? Over there by the empty bag of peanuts. Undershirt? I'm wearing that. Pants: unzipped and belt missing, but still on legs. Shoes and socks: tossed aside near the door. A little messy, but everything seems to be in order.

Clifford's inventory check was interrupted by a very loud noise that sounded vaguely like a Harley starting up. At first his battered brain couldn't identify the source, but gradually it dawned on him that the most important man in the global diamond industry was sleeping soundly not three feet away. Clifford forced himself upright, waited for the rush of wooziness to pass, and tried to remember: what the hell happened last night?

CHAPTER 25

Gaborone, 5:45 a.m.

There would be time to piece together yesterday's events, but for now the primary objective was to get out of the presidential suite as quickly as possible. Clifford held his pants up with one hand, and grabbed his shirt, shoes and socks with the other. Ever so quietly he made his way to the door, forced his discarded clothing into his left hand, and with his right slowly turned the handle and stepped across the threshold. Breathing a sigh of relief he then turned around to face the door, dropped his clothes in the hall, and with his right hand pulled the door shut very, very slowly. When at long last the latch clicked softly into place, Clifford looked up as if to thank the heavens for getting him out of this mess reasonably intact. He then bent over to retrieve his shirt, shoes and socks, and begin the Walk of Shame back to his own room.

As he straightened up he nearly bumped into the man standing just six inches away, a man who caused Clifford's heart to stop by saying an overly cheery "good morning!" It was the worst possible person to meet in this situation: Charles Lithwick.

Lithwick had worked at Delacroix for nearly 17 years. He was considered reasonably competent, but certainly not a star. Unfortunately, years of annual feedback sessions had failed to make a dent in Lithwick's self-confidence, and when the position of Deputy Sales Director opened up he was sure the role was his. So sure, in fact, he made a point of quite publicly telling anyone who would listen that he would get the job.

Lithwick didn't take the resulting disappointment well. In a series of e-mails to colleagues – all of which Delacroix made effective use of in the resulting court case – he claimed he was the victim of corruption. Said that the Sales Director had received regular additions to the wine cellar he kept with Berry Bros. & Rudd, all of them gifts from the man who was ultimately given the job. Lithwick admitted there was no physical evidence, but claimed to have it "on good authority". The lack of evidence, he explained, proved nothing more than that the cover-up had been very effective.

Delacroix management comes from hardy stock, and is willing to allow a certain amount of spleen to be vented, provided it is done appropriately and over with reasonably quickly. Written allegations of bribery are an entirely different matter, however, and Lithwick was called to account. The Head of Human Resources told him he was in violation of the Disparagement & Disrepute clause in his contract, and asked him to leave the building immediately. Lithwick replied that if he did so, his next stop would be at his lawyer's office.

The court case was over nearly as soon as it began. For starters, Lithwick didn't actually have a lawyer, and by the time he found one he could afford there was very little time left before the first hearing. Then the plaintiff was intimidated

– as expected – when Delacroix showed up with not one but six lawyers, each looking more sinister than the next. When the judge realized Lithwick had no evidence supporting his claims, and Delacroix had written proof of the public allegations, he quickly ruled in favor of the defendant.

Lithwick hadn't really expected to win, but he had expected Delacroix to settle rather than see their name sullied in the court of public opinion. When the verdict went against him he suddenly realized the bigger issue was what the public now thought of *him*, particularly the part that works in the diamond industry. It wasn't a good career move to unsuccessfully sue the world's biggest diamond company; no potential employer wanted to shackle themselves with an irritant to The Giant. He was, as they say, radioactive.

Lithwick lived off his savings for nearly nine months, until suddenly he had a brainstorm. While almost everyone in the industry was afraid of the superior firepower wielded by Delacroix, there was one party who might *want* someone who understood The Firm intimately, knew its strength, but was nonetheless unafraid and eager to do battle. That party was the Government of Botswana.

Publicly the 50/50 joint venture between Delacroix and the Government of Botswana had been hailed as a masterstroke of resource management and appropriate partnership. South Africa, where Delacroix owns 100% of all its mines, spoke with envy about the "Botswana model". And between payments for the diamonds, taxes, and their share of profits from the various joint ventures, Government took more than 90 cents out of every dollar generated by Delacroix in Botswana.

But behind the scenes, the Botswana side was dangerously unhappy. They had seen how much a diamond sells for in Tiffany's on Fifth Avenue in New York City, compared that with the price Delacroix paid them for a rough diamond, and concluded they'd been ripped off – for the last four decades.

Increasingly aggressive negotiating tactics had resulted in small improvements in the terms of their agreement with Delacroix, but the country was almost out of time. The best estimates are that Botswana will run out of diamonds by 2030 and when that happens, half of government revenue will simply vanish. The means the country has less than 20 years to get enough money out of Delacroix to pay for a new economy *not* dangerously dependent on one natural resource.

The government needed a game changer, someone who could show them where the bodies were buried, and help them gain the upper hand in their negotiations with Delacroix. After years of searching, they finally found their man.

Charles Lithwick.

The first time he walked into the negotiating room and took a seat on the Botswana side of the table, there was an audible gasp. This moved the battle to a completely different level, one certain to be more intense and far more personal than anything that had gone before it. Those on the Delacroix side expecting the worst were not disappointed. Lithwick had spent nearly two months digging up every slight Botswana had suffered in their 45-year relationship with the company, and pulled one out whenever the government appeared to be losing ground. However Delacroix had been through this sort of war before, and wasn't as easily knocked off its stride as Government had hoped. As the increasingly rancorous negotiating sessions dragged on, it became clear that while Lithwick had enough dirt to score a large number of points, he didn't have a knockout blow.

Until he bumped into Clifford Watkins coming out of the Presidential Suite at the Grand Palm Resort and Casino, holding up his pants and carrying his shoes, shirt and socks.

CHAPTER 26

Gaborone, 5:47 a.m.

"Good morning. I must say you look rather familiar, but I'm not sure we've met. It does appear, however that you have – shall we say – 'met' the chairman."

Clifford's face went from greenish-blue to a bright red. "I don't know what you're insinuating."

"I'm not insinuating anything. I'm *saying* I find it interesting a Delacroix employee was seen coming out of Mr. Weil's bedroom at – what time is it now? – just before 6 in the morning."

"That doesn't mean a thing."

"Most people would likely agree with you...if it weren't for the fact you're half-naked."

"Get your mind out of the gutter."

"My mind thinks only the purest thoughts. But it is struggling to come up with an innocent explanation for the position we currently find you in."

"Look: I got drunk. I fell asleep. Now I'm awake and heading back to my room. That's all there is to it."

"You're young, but surely you're not *that* innocent, are you? After all, I assume you know who I am?"

"Of course I do. You're that guy who lost it after he didn't get promoted, tried to sue the company, got creamed, and then tried to get revenge by telling the Botswana Government every bit of malicious gossip you ever heard during your time at Delacroix."

"Perhaps not the way I would have phrased it, but you've got the gist about right. Let's focus, shall we, on that last bit."

"You mean the bit about the gossip?"

"That's the one! If you're right that I'm trying to bring down the House of Weil with tales told out of school, how do you think this little encounter is making me feel?"

Clifford's blood ran cold. Even an impartial observer would admit this scene didn't look very good – for the company, for the chairman, or for Clifford. But Charles Lithwick was far from impartial, and Clifford had just handed him the ammunition with which to blow up Delacroix.

"You've got nothing," Clifford bluffed. "I'll admit I look a little ridiculous, but unless you're about to pull out a camera no one will ever know that but the two of us. As for anything that you think may or may not have happened last night, you've got no proof of anything."

"Proof? This isn't about proof. It's about creativity. Let's see. What about 'Diamond King Caught in Rent Boy Sting'? No? The rhyme is a bit *déclassé*? What about 'Africa's Richest Man Caught in Homo Love Nest'? 'Diamond World Not the

Only Thing Weil Tops?' Ok, I admit those aren't great. You caught me by surprise. Give me some time and I'll come up with some truly cringe-worthy stuff that the *Botswana Guardian* would kill to put on their front page."

"You wouldn't dare!"

"Why not? It wouldn't be the first time the *Guardian* has got a story slightly wrong."

"But it would humiliate the chairman, and the company. How could he walk into the negotiations when everyone on the other side of table is holding a copy of that slander?"

"Ah, Bambi grows up. Isn't that wonderful, boys and girls? Too bad Mother had to be burnt to a crisp first in that awful, awful fire."

"I'll tell everyone it isn't true. I'll say I got drunk and fell asleep; that's all there was to it."

"Go ahead and type it up. I'll even deliver it to the *Guardian* for you. Given how little content they've got, they'll probably print it. On page 12, of course, along with the other corrections like "we reported the price of chicken at Folger's Market was 45 pula per pound, while the correct price is 55 pula. The *Guardian* regrets the error."

"Have you no shame?"

"I've thought about that quite a bit, and decided the answer is no, I don't. Must have left it on my desk the day I got fired and was forced to leave the office immediately like a common criminal."

"Delacroix has lawyers to stop people like you."

"And the Government of Botswana has lawyers to protect me. I'm quite a valuable asset, you know. A diamond expert with inside knowledge of Delacroix and a violent dislike for the company. That makes me a rock star on Team Botswana."

"I can't believe what you're saying to me. No wonder Delacroix fired you."

"Just so. But enough about me. I haven't even asked your name."

"Ask all you want. I'm not going to tell you."

"Now, now. There's no reason to be childish about this. There must be 100 people at this conference who know who you are, and I know most of them. All I need do is ask and your identity would be revealed, Batman. So why don't you save us both some time and just tell me."

It was hard to argue with Lithwick's logic. More important, Clifford had to get out of this hall quickly, before someone else saw him holding his pants together at his hips. "Clifford Watkins," he said, practically spitting with contempt.

"See – that wasn't so hard, was it? It was nice meeting you Clifford. I'll be in touch to discuss our... arrangement." And with that Lithwick walked down the hall and onto a waiting elevator.

Clifford ran down the hall to the emergency stairs, threw on his shirt, buttoned up his pants, and stepped into his shoes without taking time to put on his socks. He rushed down two flights to his own floor, checked that no one was coming, and then made a dash for his room. 6:25. He barely had time for a quick shower before he needed to be in the breakfast room for the daily briefing.

He never saw the maid standing outside the door next to his, her face a picture of puzzlement mixed with more than a trace of shock.

CHAPTER 27

Antwerp, February 20, 11 a.m.

"Daniel, I'm sorry to disturb you while you're cutting, but there's a man at the door who insists on seeing you."

"Jesus, Brigitte, can't you see I've got my hands full?"

"I said I'm sorry. But when I told him you were busy he just smiled. Didn't say a word. To tell you the truth, he scared me."

In that moment, Daniel knew exactly who was waiting at the entrance to his workshop. And suddenly he, too, felt frightened.

"Ok, ok, tell him I'll be right there."

But Daniel didn't leave his workbench immediately. He took his time putting down his tools, thinking about how he was going to handle this unexpected and very unwelcome development. It would be a lot easier to come up with a strategy, he thought, if he had even a vague idea of what the thug was doing here. Well, guessing wouldn't help; ultimately he had no choice but to ask. He made his way up the staircase from the workroom to the reception area, taking deep breaths and trying to calm his tap-dancing nerves.

"Hello, Daniel."

"Hello, Frans. I'm rather surprised to see you here."

"And here I was thinking you'd be pleased."

"Is there something I can help you with?"

"I just dropped by to see how work on our diamond is proceeding."

"*Our* diamond?" Daniel asked, in genuine surprise.

"Of course. I did tell you we'd be buying it back once polished, didn't I?"

Frans had said nothing of the sort; Daniel was certain of that. And he was just as certain Frans knew it, too. It was like playing poker with your eyes closed: only the other side really knew what was happening.

"Why would you want to do that?", Daniel asked in a desperate attempt to buy time.

"That's how we always work. Sell the rough at a good price, and buy back the resulting polish. We did give you a good price, didn't we Daniel?"

"Yes, yes, of course. Very good. Thank you. But how can you promise to buy the polish before it's done? Even I can't be sure what size the diamond will be, much less the quality."

"That's a good point, Daniel, a very good point. But we can sort all that out once we've seen the finished product."

"Can I assume you'll pay the full Rap price?"

"Of course not. No one pays full Rap, especially in this market. We were thinking Rap less 30."

"30% off? That's a very substantial discount, especially for a stone as special as this one will be."

"But you'll be lucky to sell at all, Daniel. You've known all along it wasn't – what shall I call it – a *normal* diamond, haven't you?"

At that moment, the scales fell from Daniel's eyes. There was a reason they'd picked him above all the better, more famous cutters of large stones. There was a reason they offered him a below-market price on a truly exceptional piece of rough. There was a reason Achmed Khalif not only knew who he was, but was expecting his visit. It had been a setup from the very beginning.

"What's wrong with it?"

"Nothing, Daniel, nothing. I'm sure you've seen that it is of excellent quality, with a high potential yield."

"What's wrong with it?" Daniel asked again, surprising himself with his vehemence.

"As a diamond, absolutely nothing. As an international commodity, it might be lacking a document or two."

Daniel's mind raced through the possibilities. The stone could be from somewhere like Zimbabwe or Ivory Coast, countries that hadn't been approved by the Kimberley Process that governs the international trade in rough. That would make it subject to confiscation... but only until polished. And Daniel was already well down the road with that.

It could have been smuggled. Lots of that going on in Zimbabwe, Sierra Leone, the Congo. That would be dangerous for the people doing the actual smuggling, but once the goods crossed the border it was nearly impossible to prove where they'd come from – much less that they hadn't been reported.

It could be stolen. Large polished stones are relatively easy to trace, using the grading paperwork. But Daniel had bought rough, and already it looked nothing like it did when he first took possession.

Once again, Daniel found himself with no better option than asking the obvious – but potentially dangerous – question: "What documents are missing?"

"Daniel, Daniel, Daniel. Do you really want to ask me that sort of question – especially when you can answer it yourself?"

Daniel swallowed hard. He hadn't insisted on Kimberley Process certificates, as he was required to do by law. He wanted to believe he simply forgot in the excitement of being offered such an exceptional diamond at such a ridiculous price. But as he tried that excuse on for size, he realized he'd known all along that he was cheating.

He also realized that it would be almost impossible for him to sell the polished diamond. He didn't know anyone who could afford to buy a stone this size. If he started asking around, there would be talk about how little Danny Stern had gotten his hands on a big boy's diamond. The end customer might not ask whether the diamond came with a Kimberley certificate, but then again, he might. If that happened he would be exposed… and stuck with a diamond he'd paid $1.5 million for and couldn't resell.

Achmed Khalif would not like that.

Frans watched Daniel work his way through the mental obstacle course, and smiled when the color left Daniel's face. "Can I assume we have a deal?"

CHAPTER 28

Gaborone, March 21, 10:15 a.m.

Detective TH Mabusla stood at near-attention. His boss, Chief Inspector Ohilwe, pushed himself away from his desk, clasped his hands behind his head, and in the gentlest voice he could manage asked "So, how did it go?"

"Not as well as one could have hoped. Inspector McLean is nobody's fool."

"Did he buy the idea that foreign mercenaries might have had something to do with the death of the former head of Delacroix Botswana?"

TH considered his response carefully. "I don't think he *doesn't* believe it."

"Would you mind untangling all those negatives for me?"

"I think he sees Moeng's death as a side show, an interesting coincidence but not something that will help him solve *his* case."

Chief Ohilwe got up from his chair and walked over to the window. "We need rain."

TH said nothing.

Still looking at the window, the Chief continued. "I'm told there was an interesting article in the most recent edition of *Diamond Insider*. It speculated that a South African hit squad was responsible for Sammy's premature demise. Any idea where they might have got that from?"

"None, sir."

The Chief kept his back turned towards Mabusla.

"Now that I think about it, sir, isn't that article a good thing? After all, it supports the line we took with McLean."

"Yes, that is a rather fortunate coincidence, isn't it?"

"Indeed it is, sir."

Ohilwe allowed himself a tiny smile, and then returned to his desk. "Does McLean have a suspect?"

"Other than us?"

"What would make you say something like that? It's a perfectly innocent question."

"The problem is, sir, that McLean doesn't think we're all that innocent. When I dropped him off at the Palm, he thanked me for calling him in, and said it was good to finally be working *together* with the Botswana police."

"Meaning he doesn't have the same warm and fuzzy relationship with Detective Motswagae."

"No, sir."

"And that's got him wondering *why* – especially since, in theory at least, we're both on the same side."

"Precisely, sir. And I'm worried about the collateral damage once this rather large bull starts scurrying around the china shop, looking for something before he even knows what it is. That would be dangerous at the best of times. And these are not the best of times."

The Chief's eyes narrowed. "We have no idea whether our government was involved in either the incident in London, or the death of Sammy Moeng. Until we do, your job is to keep Inspector McLean occupied with ends that are dead and goose chases that are decidedly wild. He can't destroy the china shop if you don't let him inside."

So now it's all on *my* shoulders, TH thought with rising anger. Too bad *I* don't have a subordinate to dump this on. Trying to keep the irritation out of his voice, TH mounted a counterattack. "How do we know this has anything to do with Botswana?"

"I would have thought a note in the dead man's pocket saying REMEMBER GABORONE is a pretty good indication."

"But what if that was just to throw the police off the scent by getting them out of London and into southern Africa where they don't know anyone or understand anything? After all, the body was found in the company's London office, not its Botswana operations. If you want to link Delacroix and Botswana, why not commit the crime here?"

Chief Ohilwe let the question bounce around in his head for a bit. "Perhaps because it's easier? The killer would have had a hard time getting a gun here. As long as the total prohibition on handgun licenses remains in effect, the only way to get a pistol is to steal it from a select number of police officers like you and me who are allowed to carry. And we would report the theft immediately."

TH looked unimpressed. "From what I can remember Britain has pretty strict rules on firearms, too. I think the only way you can have a pistol is if you keep it at a gun club."

Both men sat in silence for several minutes. TH developed a sudden, keen interest in the length of his fingernails, which he continued to examine as he began speaking. "What if the message wasn't *to* Botswana, but *from* it?"

"I haven't the foggiest notion what you're talking about."

"Chief, I'm not saying this is what happened. I'm not even suggesting it. I'm just thinking out loud about a possibility." TH looked to the ceiling for support. "Right now our government is negotiating a new mining contract with Delacroix. According to the paper, it's likely to be worth $3 - $3.5 billion a year for the next 10 years. That's a lot of money, about half the government's budget. So if the BDP wants to keep its stranglehold on power, it needs to beat Delacroix in the negotiations. Maybe someone involved in that process wanted to tip the scales a bit."

"Are you seriously suggesting our government killed a man as a negotiating tactic?"

"I'm merely saying that it falls within the realm of the theoretically possible. After all, we're talking about a huge amount of money. And a huge amount of power. That makes people do all kinds of strange things."

"I'd hardly call murder a 'strange thing'."

"You know what I mean, Chief. Maybe someone on our side knows a secret or two about Delacroix that they think they can use for leverage."

"A few gentle hints dropped into the negotiations at the right moment would probably have made the point. No need to kill anyone, especially in such a flashy manner."

"You're probably right."

"I usually am. But until we are absolutely certain that no one in government was involved in either incident, we have to assume the worst and plan accordingly. That means treading very carefully. Towards that end I suggest you make Inspector McLean think you are a kind, accommodating but ultimately fairly incompetent police officer."

Mabusla grinned. "I did some acting at university, but I'm not sure even I could make such an obvious lie seem believable."

Ohilwe briefly raised one eyebrow before returning to the mound of papers on his desk, signaling the discussion was over.

CHAPTER 29

Gaborone, March 19, 7:14 p.m.

With no enthusiasm whatsoever, an exhausted Inspector McLean unlocked the door to his room, grabbed a Windhoek beer out of the mini-fridge, and collapsed onto the bed. Today had been full of more surprises than a man his age should have to deal with.

Mystery #1 was why a former director of Delacroix Mining ended up with a bullet in his brain and his body torn apart by wild animals. Detective Mabusla had said the director was the richest man in Botswana. Owned not one but two Ferraris in a country with so few paved roads even a Mini could cover them all in the better part of a morning. That was certain to inspire envy, perhaps even anger. After all, despite the economic miracle Botswana still had high unemployment and a very uneven distribution of wealth. Who could blame the man in the street for resenting someone with so much more than they could ever dream of?

But that sort of thinking usually leads to robbery, not murder. That was Mystery #2. Even standing above the body, McLean could see the victim was still wearing what looked to be a very expensive watch. Perhaps the killer had been scared off, but the body had been found in one of the most remote locations McLean had ever seen. The odds of someone stumbling onto a crime in progress were almost infinitesimally low. And what about the wallet? Yes, what *about* the wallet? McLean would need to check whether it had been on the body.

And that brought him neatly to Mystery #3. The whole time he'd been in this country, the local police had been polite, but not exactly helpful. Then all of a sudden he gets a call inviting him to the initial inspection of a crime that may have absolutely nothing to do with his own case. Why? Who benefits from getting him involved? Was it a red herring, designed to distract him from the primary investigation? Or was someone in the police department trying to point him in the right direction, without being seen to do so?

Only one way to find out...

"This is Inspector McLean of Scotland Yard, calling for Detective Motswagae."

"Just a moment please...."

As McLean waited for the detective to come to the phone, he thought through the various ways to play this call. While Motswagae might be awed by the sight of the Inspector at full gallop on his high horse, McLean doubted indignation was the way to go. With men who dislike direct confrontation, it's almost always better to remain calm, respectful and – if at all possible – upbeat. That wasn't the Inspector's best role, but perhaps he could manage it over the phone.

"Inspector, how can I help you today?"

Gaborone, March 19, 7:14 p.m.

"Detective, I have had a most interesting day, thanks to your colleagues up north."

"I'm glad to hear we were of service."

"Would you care to hear what that service was?"

"Only if you wish to tell me, Inspector."

"I do, Detective Motswagae, as I think today may have been a turning point in my case." McLean paused for a few seconds to let the tension build. "Were you aware that the body of Sammy Moeng, former MD of Delacroix Mining, was found in the Tuli Block, having been shot and then mauled by wild animals?"

"Yes, Inspector, I was, although I think the order of those two events is still a subject of some debate – at least according to the report that came across my desk a few hours ago."

"What did you think when you saw it?"

"I'm not sure I understand the question."

"Then let me rephrase it. Did you find it surprising that a man with the closest of ties to the company that figures prominently in my investigation died in suspicious circumstances during my short stay in your country?"

"I did think it was a rather remarkable coincidence. But wild animal attacks are still quite common here."

"I have no doubt what you say is true, but it doesn't explain the gunshot behind his ear."

"No, Inspector, it does not." McLean paused to admire the way Motswagae managed to address the question without actually answering it. If he hadn't become a policeman, the man would have done very well on the other side of the table in an Interpol interrogation room.

"The reason I'm calling, Detective, isn't just to discuss today's news. I was wondering if you could check the case file for me and let me know whether the victim still had his wallet."

"Excuse me?"

"His wallet. Was it still on the body? And if so, was the money still there?"

"Why do you ask?"

"Because I noticed the victim still had his watch. I'm no expert, but it looked very expensive – a Rolex, perhaps."

"And you're wondering why the killer didn't steal it."

"Precisely."

"Perhaps the killer was frightened off by the animals that attacked the body."

"I'll grant you that's possible."

"Or maybe the lethal shot was fired from a distance, and the killer was never near the body. Were you able to check the entry wound for powder burns?

"Not yet." Strictly speaking that was true. The vultures had made such a mess of the victim's face there were no clues visible to the naked eye. But Detective Mabusla had called about an hour ago to say the initial draft of the forensics report would say the lethal shot had been fired from a

Gaborone, March 19, 7:14 p.m.

distance of less than three feet. For now, at least, McLean chose not to share that finding.

"If you're right and the shot was fired from a distance too great to be robbery, what's your theory about motive?"

"I don't have one, Inspector. I am simply trying to separate what we *know* from what we're merely guessing about. We don't yet have enough facts to start speculating as to the killer's motivation."

Once again McLean noticed how careful – cagey, even – Motswagae was being. Perhaps that was just a copper's natural inclination to avoid jumping to conclusions. Maybe the man didn't want McLean thinking he could be pushed around. Maybe it was just the natural reserve of the Batswana. Or maybe the man suspected – as McLean did – that Moeng had been assassinated to keep him quiet.

That wasn't terribly surprising. Someone in his position probably knew a lot of things that could get him killed, and according to Mabusla, Sammy Moeng had the sort of grandiose personality that would tell tales out of school in order to impress his listeners. That meant there were probably a lot of people who were glad to see him dead.

Fortunately, the list of people who might have pulled the trigger was considerably shorter.

To get within three feet of the victim, the shooter must have either been someone Moeng knew – or an authority figure by whom he was intimidated if not actually frightened. Like a soldier. Or a policeman. McLean decided to keep that thought to himself.

"Detective, has there ever been any talk about Delacroix, Delacroix Mining or Moeng himself being involved with illicit contributions to the Botswana Democratic Party?"

"The opposition papers are full of such stories, but they have yet to provide an iota of proof."

"So you think the stories are baseless?"

"I think that until I see supporting evidence, it's all just idle gossip."

"Let's assume for a moment not everyone is as fair and sensible as you are. Let's say – just for the sake of argument – that where there's smoke there's fire, and the stories *are* true. Would the fallout from them going public be sufficient to justify killing Moeng to ensure his silence?"

"There's never a justification for murder," Motswagae said sanctimoniously.

"I know, Detective, I know. But we're not talking about right and wrong here, we're talking about what might motivate a killer."

Detective Motswagae took a very long time before answering. "I would say there are a large number of people – both here and abroad – who are very glad Sammy Moeng is dead."

"I see. Well thank you for your help, Detective. In my final report I'll be sure to mention the support provided by both you and Detective Mabulsa. Oh, by the way, did you happen to speak to him today?"

"Why do you ask, Inspector?"

"I was just wondering whether he had filled you in on today's events." And judging from your evasive non-answer it's very clear he did, thought McLean as he hung up the phone. Now why would Motswagae want to hide that?

CHAPTER 30

London, Three Years Earlier

Clifford didn't sleep a wink on the flight back from London. A few drinks too many and suddenly he had put the future of a storied company in jeopardy. While the chairman might worry about creating headlines in Botswana, Clifford was worried about being front-page fodder for the UK tabloids. "Empire Crumbles: One Man To Blame". "120 Years Of Glory Ends In Single Night of Debauchery". Sex, money and power destroyed? For Fleet Street this was as irresistible a combination as bangers and mash.

As he sat in the cab on the way from Heathrow to his small flat in Putney, Clifford briefly convinced himself that if he just disappeared off the face of the earth, Lithwick would have no choice but to move on. But just as he started to feel comfortable with the idea of life on the run, he suddenly realized this wasn't about him at all. Lithwick was bent on destroying the company that – as the Americans would say – had done him wrong, and Clifford was just a bit player in that particular drama. If anything, a disappearance would give the slander the ring of truth.

Clifford stood under a scalding-hot shower, flailing his skin in what he thought was well-deserved punishment for his stupidity. Could he have handled the hallway encounter better than he did? Of course, but that sort of thing is obvious only in hindsight. At the time he was surprised, half-awake, semi-naked and badly hung over; no one does his best work under those circumstances. Besides, what's done is done. All that remains is to make the best of a bad situation. No, a very bad situation. The worst. A catastrophe of unparalleled degree. And after two full days thinking of nothing else, he'd come to the conclusion there was no escape. He was simply going to have to man up, tell the chairman what had happened, and let the chips fall as they may.

He exited Farringdon Tube Station, and walked towards the Thames until he reached a Prêt a Manger shop. There he ordered two triple espressos, and half a smoked salmon and cream cheese sandwich he hoped would keep the caffeine from burning a hole in his stomach. He consumed the food and drink slowly, tasting neither. Finally both cups had been drained and the last crumbs from the sandwich picked up with a licked finger. Clifford had run out of delaying tactics; it was time to face the proverbial music.

The short walk to the Delacroix building seemed to take every ounce of energy he had. As he flashed his ID at Security, and then again at the sensor on the right side of the huge doors protecting the elevator hall, he remembered the excitement he'd felt the first time he'd entered this building – for the interview that got him the job he had now put at risk. He remembered how awed he was to be allowed past the third set of electronically locked doors, and into the belly of the beast. He remembered getting into the ancient elevator, and thinking a company with as much money as Delacroix

London, Three Years Earlier

should be able to afford the occasional office refurbishment. He remembered how an old family friend had seduced him with tales of far-away lands, and how badly he wanted to be a part of those stories.

Once he had been. His days in Africa would forever be the highlight of his life. And while those days were already behind him, a victim of changes in corporate direction, it wasn't until today he truly felt they were over. Clifford of Africa had reached the end of the road.

He found a deserted conference room far from his desk, shut the door, and made the call.

"Chairman's office."

"Um, hello. This is Clifford Watkins. In Sales. Downstairs. I want... I need to speak with the chairman urgently."

"I'm afraid he's tied up at the moment. Can I ask what this is referring to?"

"It's a, um, confidential matter."

"I see. Well the first opening he has is June 6 at 2 PM for 20 minutes."

"That's nearly 3 months away!"

"The chairman is a very busy man."

"I realize that. I'm sorry. I forgot myself for a minute there. But this is both urgent and important, and I'm sure after the chairman sees me he'll be glad you found a way to fit me in. I only need 15 minutes... 10 if must be. It really is a critical matter."

"Mr. Watkins, I'd be happy to ask the chairman if he's willing to cancel something on his schedule in order to meet with you, but the first thing he'll ask me is what it's about."

"Tell him it's, um, about output from the Future Vision session in Gaborone. About the – uh - discussion we had on the second night."

"Ok, I'll tell him that and get back to you with his response. Cheers for now."

Cheers. Jesus Christ. The last thing Clifford wanted now was to be reminded of alcohol.

Twenty minutes later his phone rang. "Clifford, it's Julia Collins. The chairman's meeting finished ahead of schedule, so if you can get up here right away, he can give you 10 minutes."

Clifford literally ran up the stairs, and was still short of breath when he reached the reception area. "That was quick," said Julia. "I'll take you in."

This was the first time Clifford had ever walked across the threshold and into the office of the most powerful man in the global diamond industry. It was large, though not massive. Simply decorated. Surprisingly free of any personal effects. Except for the man sitting behind the large teak desk, there was nothing intimidating or threatening about it.

"Good morning, Clifford. It's nice to see you."

"And you, sir. Thank you for taking time to see me."

"Would you like a coffee? Julia, a tea for me, please."

London, Three Years Earlier

"No thank you, sir. If you don't mind I'd like to jump right in. Before I start having second thoughts."

"Sounds serious."

"I'm afraid it is, sir."

"Well in that case, the floor is yours."

"Sir, do you remember the second night of the Future Vision conference in Gaborone? You and I had a long chat, and I had far too much to drink."

The chairman said nothing, but nodded his head ever so slightly.

"Well, I must have fallen asleep in your room, and when I left early the next morning I bumped into someone in the hallway."

Another nod, this one encouraging Clifford to pick up the pace.

"Charles Lithwick."

For the first time the chairman's eyes showed something other than slight impatience. Clifford wasn't exactly sure what he saw: maybe caution, maybe rising anger, possibly fear.

"Did he tell you what he was doing in the hotel at that hour of the morning? I seem to recall he lives in Gaborone, so he shouldn't have need of a hotel room."

Clifford fell back in his chair. "I don't know, sir. And to be completely honest, it never occurred to me to ask."

The chairman shrugged, as if no longer interested in the question.

"It gets worse, sir. I was so embarrassed to have passed out on your sofa that I ran out of the room, not... um... fully dressed."

"I see. And did our former colleague have anything to say about that?"

"He did, sir. He said he would tell the Botswana press what he'd seen, and they'd be sure to turn it into a scandal."

"And how did you respond?"

"I said he had no proof."

"And he said proof has nothing to do with it."

"Precisely, sir."

"And what did you say in response to his threat?"

"I said I'd set the record straight. He laughed at me, and said even if I did get a retraction they'd put it in the back of the paper where no one would see it."

"He could well be right about that. We're not exactly popular in Botswana at this point in the contract negotiations."

"Sir, I'm terribly, terribly sorry. I know I should have handled it differently - somehow - but I was so surprised at being caught like that, and then being threatened, that I just couldn't think straight."

Clifford was crushing his left hand with his right, as if hoping to squeeze the sin from his body. "Don't be too hard on yourself. Charles Lithwick is a specialist in lobbing hand grenades. There's usually very little one can do but keep one's head down and pray one doesn't get blown to bits."

"Sir, is there any chance he's just a bully who will back off if we show him we're not afraid of his threats? Maybe if we threaten to sue him, or reveal his tactics publicly, he'll just back down. If you think that's the right way to go, I'd be happy to testify. I don't care what people think of me; I just want to do the right thing for the company."

The chairman was silent for a full minute. "Clifford, that's very noble of you. As was bringing this to me right away. I'm sure it couldn't have been easy, and I appreciate the courage it took to come here. As for Next Steps, I'm not sure involving Legal – and creating piles of documents that fly around the office before landing God knows where – is the best way to proceed. In my experience this sort of situation is best resolved through direction negotiations between the principals.

"I'm not sure I understand, sir."

"Charles Lithwick cares exclusively about Charles Lithwick. We must figure out what he wants, and give it to him."

"But that's blackmail!"

"I prefer to think of it as a negotiation. Have you got any idea what Lithwick wants in exchange for his silence?"

A brief glimmer of hope popped into Clifford's head. "He said he would be in touch to discuss what comes next."

"Perfect. Wait for his call, listen to what he has to say, and then we can meet again to plot our response."

"Yes, sir."

"Chin up, Clifford. The world won't end tomorrow."

Maybe not for you, Clifford thought despondently as he made his way out the door.

CHAPTER 31

Gaborone, March 20, 7:30 P.M.

While talking with Thoko at the casino had been useful, the Inspector felt he really needed to speak with her brother. So he invited the two of them for a steak dinner at the Grand Palm's Beef Baron restaurant, determined to list them as "social worker and her associate" in his expense report.

He got there early so he'd have time to study the wine list carefully, and convert all the prices from pula to pounds sterling before making a selection. That didn't take nearly as long as he'd planned – a bottle of Seven Sisters Pinotage from South Africa quickly caught his eye, and was reasonably priced – so he leaned back in his chair and surveyed his surroundings.

The décor was an unsuccessful mix of European dark paneling, bush lamps, and wicker-backed chairs that seemed to be on permanent loan from the pool deck. It felt like a British men's club designed by someone who not only had never been to England but who was forced for budgetary reasons to shop at a patio supply store. But there was one completely local touch that McLean found very promising if a bit unnerving: steak knives larger and sharper than anything he'd ever seen outside a murder investigation.

It was at that very moment Thoko and her brother walked into the restaurant. She was even more stunning than he'd remembered, especially since her trashy working clothes had been replaced by a simple, elegant knee-length dress. Her brother was equally good looking, despite the hesitation written across his face. Fortunately, Thoko took the reins.

"Inspector, this is my brother, Peter. Peter, this is Inspector McLean of Scotland Yard."

The detective reached out his hand. "Please call me Ian. And thanks very much for coming."

Peter shrugged. "It's hard to say no to my sister."

McLean let his eyes do a second tour of Thoko's elegant body, and thought "ain't that the truth".

The three were seated, and McLean tried to make small talk. After several embarrassing failures – "Is it always so hot here?" was probably the most humiliating – he abandoned all pretense and began the interrogation. "Your sister tells me you work for Delacroix."

"For the joint venture, actually: Delacroix Diamond Trading."

"What do you do for them?"

"I'm a sorter."

"Which means...?"

Peter took a deep breath while he thought about how to tell a very long and complicated story in just a few sentences. "Every day about a million rough diamonds come into the

Gaborone, March 20, 7:30 P.M.

sorting house. Our job is to separate them by weight, color, and clarity so they can be priced for sale."

"A million a day? I thought diamonds were rare."

"They are. All those diamonds together weigh only a little more than 25 kilograms. And most of them are the very small diamonds you see on the sides of rings – not the big stone in the middle."

"Is it difficult work?"

"Not really. It only takes a few months to learn how to do it. The tough part is looking for tiny differences in very similar stones, eight hours a day. Some days by the time I get home my eyes hurt so much I want to pull them out of my head."

"So that's what makes a good sorter – good eyesight?"

"That's part of it. But patience is probably more important."

A waitress with a backside nearly as large as their table asked whether they wanted drinks. "Please, go ahead" McLean said. "This one's on the Queen." That little falsehood seemed to relax Peter considerably, and he ordered a glass of white wine for his sister and a beer for himself.

The Inspector decided to press his advantage. "Peter, I'm not sure if Thoko told you, but I'm trying to learn more about the security systems at Delacroix for a murder investigation" – another deliberate but almost certainly helpful exaggeration – "I'm working on in England. This is my identification; if you'd like to speak to someone at Scotland

Yard to confirm I'm who I say I am, you're welcome to use my phone."

Peter's smile was a clone of Thoko's. "That won't be necessary. Sis says you're legit, and even if you're not you're paying for dinner and that's good enough for me."

"Thank you. I need your help because, to be completely honest, we're stumped. You may have read that a few days ago there was an incident at the Delacroix head office at #42 Farringdon Road in London. I can't go into the details, other to say – and this must stay between us – the security system has no record of either the victim or the perpetrator entering the building. I'm trying to understand how that could happen."

Peter first looked stunned, and then laughed. "Wait a minute: someone snuck *in* to Delacroix?"

"Unbelievable, I know. But in order to figure out how they did it, I need to know how to get things *out*."

"It's almost impossible." Peter shook his head in amusement, then pointed at his sister. "She told you about the pat-downs, the strip-searches, the X-rays and all that?"

"She did."

"So you know it's not easy."

"But she also told me you accidentally took a diamond out of the building, meaning the system isn't foolproof."

Peter shot a less-than-happy look at his sister. "Did she also tell you my whole team had to spend four hours looking for the damn thing? And if I hadn't brought it back the next day they would have subtracted the cost from everyone's pay."

"How did they know it was missing?"

"Every time the diamonds get moved, they're weighed. If anyone even suspects there's something funny going on, they're weighed. If a supervisor just feels like covering his ass, they're weighed. And if the weight comes up short, no one leaves until the missing diamond is found."

"So would you say it's harder to get them off the sorting floor than out the door?"

"No, I'd say both are near-impossible."

"So no one has ever stolen diamonds from Delacroix Trading Company?"

Peter suddenly went quiet. He looked at his sister. She nodded. He took a deep breath, and let it out slowly. "Not exactly. There have been a couple of cases in the past few years."

"Anything recently?"

Peter nodded. "This past January. 27 carats disappeared into thin air. Security went bat-shit. And I guess top management did as well, because they fired the guy in charge."

"27 carats? That seems like a huge amount, especially given what you've said about how careful they are."

"That's why most people think it was an inside job."

"Who on the inside could get away with something like that?"

"Might be one of the supervisors. They could change the records of the weigh-ins. But my money would be on the guys in transport. They've got the best opportunity."

"Why is that?"

"Because after the diamonds leave the sorting house, they won't be checked again until they arrive at #42 in London. The shortfall would still be noticed, but the guards can blame it on the pilots, who can blame it on the UK delivery company, who could blame the guys doing the weighing at head office. None of them would be able to prove they didn't do it – much less that someone else did – but they can cause enough confusion to cover their tracks."

"Whereas if a sorter tries to steal something..."

"...it would be immediately obvious who's done it."

"If you wanted to put something *in* a shipment, could you do it?"

"Like what?"

"Don't worry about that for now; just humor me."

"Nah, man. When they're measuring weights down to ten thousandths of a carat, how is anybody going to put anything in without it getting noticed?"

How indeed, thought McLean.

At that very moment the steaks arrived. A little tougher than British beef perhaps, but very flavorful – especially

Gaborone, March 20, 7:30 P.M.

when washed down with the Seven Sisters Pinotage. And the sharp knives cut through the meat like... he decided not to finish the thought.

Thinking he had gotten about all he was going to get from Peter, McLean shifted the conversation to what it was like growing up in Botswana. Thoko was clearly very proud her little brother had landed a job with the biggest company in the country, and he wondered what her own life would have been like if she hadn't chosen the sex trade as a profession.

They talked for nearly two hours, managing to get through some passable desserts and a second bottle of the Pinotage. When McLean asked for the bill, Peter said 'excuse me' and went off to find the restroom. Thoko waited until he was out of sight, then leaned over the table in a conspiratorial way. "Well, was he helpful?"

"Very much so. Thank you for convincing him to talk to me."

"I aim to please." Thoko ran her fingers through her hair, letting them rest against the nape of her agonizingly beautiful neck. "Speaking of which, was Peter the only reason you asked us to come to dinner?"

McLean felt himself blushing. "I'd like to say 'yes', but I fear my face has given me away."

"That's nice. Every girl wants to be wanted."

"Yes, well, about that. You're clearly, uh, a very handsome woman and..."

"Handsome woman? *Handsome?* You make me sound like a guy in drag!"

"No, no, that's not what I meant at all!" Only after the words were out of his mouth did McLean see the grin on Thoko's face. He managed a small smile himself, and tried again.

"Actually, you're very beautiful. Exceptional, really. It's just that I've, you know, never…"

"Paid for it?"

"No, I mean yes. Of course not. What I meant to say was that I've never been unfaithful to my wife." At least, McLean thought ruefully, since that night in Islington with a different black woman and a different case.

"There aren't many men who can say that, Inspector, and I would know. But it's not like we're talking about running away together… are we?"

This time McLean looked for the grin before venturing a response. When he saw Thoko smiling broadly, he said "not tonight, at least. I've still got a mystery to solve."

"How do you think your wife would feel about you having a sensual massage – assuming, of course, that she never hears about it?"

What was it about this woman, McLean wondered, that turned him into a tongue-tied schoolboy? He was used to leading the conversation, but with Thoko he always felt two steps behind.

Gaborone, March 20, 7:30 P.M.

Mind you, it wasn't a bad feeling. Not at all.

"Inspector, Peter will be back in just a minute. If you want to spend some more time together, now's the time to say so."

"I do."

"Do... want to go upstairs together?"

McLean swallowed hard, looked down at his hands, and said "yes".

Three hours later he was alone again. Thoko had been incredible; there was no other word for it. He, on the other hand, had been a disappointment – at least the first time. But the second time had been little short of magical.

Which was not a good thing. The near-miss in Islington had clearly taught him nothing. "If you're going to fool around," he chastised himself, "at least find someone who's not involved with one of your cases.

And preferably someone on the right side of the law.

Was risk part of the attraction? McLean flashed back to his first sight of Thoko's naked body. That wasn't risk, it was lust pure and simple. Lust so strong that, for the first time in his life, he had paid a stranger for sex.

Perhaps that wasn't quite fair. Thoko wasn't really a stranger. They'd met twice, had dinner together. A lot of couples didn't wait that long before going to bed.

They also didn't pay each other for the privilege.

Jesus, McLean, what have you done? Would it have been that difficult to keep it in your pants, at least until the case had been solved?

Suddenly overwhelmed by guilt, the Inspector tried to wipe the slate clean by drowning it in work. He angrily dialed Thomas – on his home number.

"Thomas, it's me."

"Inspector! How are you, sir?"

"Fine, fine. Listen: I need you to do something for me. Can you call all of the diamond courier services, and set up an appointment with the most senior person you can find who is directly involved with the pickup and delivery of diamonds. Not someone in management who sits behind a desk all day, but a guy who's down in the trenches, who knows how the game is played."

"Certainly, sir. And what should I do after the meetings have been arranged?"

"Go to them, idiot!"

"Oh. No, sir, I mean, yes, sir, but what should I ask?"

"Ask them how they would sneak something *into* a shipment of diamonds."

"*In*, sir? Don't you mean out?"

It was at moments like this McLean wondered whether he should have been a brain surgeon, if for no other reason than to be able to remove the ones that were substandard. "If I meant out I would have said out," he said rather too sharply. "I'm developing a theory that while these companies are extremely good at preventing things from being stolen, they haven't given a minute's thought to something being *added* to a shipment."

"Like what sort of thing, sir?"

"Like a corpse. That sort of thing."

"Oh, I see. Very clever, sir. But diamonds are very small, and transported in special containers. Wouldn't a dead body stand out?"

The thought that perhaps Thomas did not possess a brain at all crossed McLean's mind. But he said only "probably."

"And wouldn't there be a manifest of some sort that the receiver checks the shipment against?"

"Almost certainly."

The young officer paused for a moment to think his way through this puzzle. "So you're thinking they had help on the inside?"

"Possibly. Maybe not a full-fledged partner. Maybe just someone who was willing to look the other way while an extra 'package' slipped through the door."

"But I thought you just said that would get noticed?"

"I'm almost certain it would. What I don't know, however, is whether anyone would care."

"Sorry, sir, I'm not following you."

"Why doesn't that surprise me? Let me phrase it another way: If someone is completely focused on not losing diamonds, they aren't paying much attention to whether something gets *added*. Surely there are times when a trusted delivery company would be asked to 'be a dear and drop this off for me'."

"True, sir, but asking someone to carry a letter is one thing. A corpse is quite another. And don't forget the pail of pig's blood."

"Dammit, I know my theory isn't airtight just yet. But if you must know, I haven't got anything else to go on right now."

McLean's rare admission of weakness left Thomas speechless. And as McLean had nothing further to say, he simply hung up the phone, lay back in bed, and found himself thinking of Thoko and the spectacular things she could do with her fingers.

CHAPTER 32

London, Three Years Earlier

The call from Lithwick came exactly one week after the early-morning encounter in the hallways of the Grand Palm Hotel. "Hello, Clifford. Are you well?"

"Let's skip the pleasantries, shall we? After all, the matter at hand is distinctly *unpleasant*."

"Now, now. There's no reason to get dramatic. Can't we just talk, one Delacroix man to another?"

"Last time I checked, you were no longer a Delacroix man."

"Touché, Clifford. And that does bring us neatly to the topic at hand."

"What do you want?"

"Let's think this through together, shall we? I have something you want, namely control of some information that would be highly embarrassing to your esteemed chairman, almost certainly end your career, and humiliate Delacroix in front of all the people of Botswana. And that would weaken the company's hand in negotiations the papers are saying are worth $30 billion. So it seems I have rather a lot that you might want. Now, what have you got that appeals to me?"

"Let me guess: money."

"Well done, old boy! Got it in one. Fabulous stuff."

"How much do you want?"

"Under the circumstances, don't you think you should make the first offer?"

"You know what our packages are like. The salary is pretty low, which they can get away with because of the generous pensions. The best I can do is 20% of my monthly pay."

Lithwick burst out laughing. "You are such an innocent. Such a pathetic little innocent. Do you really think 20% of your puny salary is enough to save one of the greatest monopolies the world has ever known?"

"I know it's not much. But it's all I can manage."

"But you're not in this alone, are you Clifford?"

It took Clifford a moment to see where Lithwick was heading. "There's no way the company is going to pay blackmail. Even if they wanted to, between the lawyers, the accountants and the auditors they'd never get away with it."

Lithwick let out another seemingly genuine belly laugh. "Clearly you don't know much about the glorious history of our exploration – or should I say exploitation? – of Africa. But no, I'm not asking for the company's involvement. I'm asking you to think a bit more creatively."

"What do you mean?"

"Clifford, I want you to resign from Delacroix."

London, Three Years Earlier

"Why? How does *that* solve anything?"

"The resignation itself doesn't. It's what comes next that counts."

"And what does come next?"

"You're going to buy a diamond mine."

"You're delusional!"

"Calm down and hear me out. You're going to buy the Orangevelt mine from Delacroix. I'll put together the financing, which God knows will be easy given that the banks are practically wetting themselves at the prospect of expanding their diamond portfolios."

"But I'm a buyer and Account Executive. I don't know the first thing about how to run a diamond mine."

"Which is precisely why I will put together your staff as well. For a mine that size seven or eight managers ought to do the trick, and miners are a dime a dozen in the current economic climate."

"So you provide the money and the people. What do I do?"

"Excellent, Clifford, excellent! For the first time today you've actually asked something sensible. A very pertinent question indeed, for it gets to the heart of our little arrangement. Your job is to buy rough diamonds from me."

"You've lost me completely. Why would I buy rough diamonds from you when I've got my own diamond mine?"

"Spot on again! You're really getting the hang of it now. Let's just say I have access to certain diamonds that lack some of the paperwork required by industry regulatory bodies."

Suddenly the light went on. "You're talking about blood diamonds..."

"Oh, Clifford, that's such a *loaded* term. I think 'paperless' sounds much better to the ear, don't you?"

"Call it whatever you want. They're still blood diamonds and it's still a violation of the Kimberley Convention to trade in them."

"Clifford, for all you know I could have bought these diamonds before the Kimberley Process was even created."

"It doesn't matter. The reality is, now that KP does exist, you can't trade those stones."

"Unless I find them a home somewhere that will provide the poor dears with the paperwork they need."

"Wait a minute. You want me to clean the diamonds for you..."

"...by mixing in them in with whatever bits and pieces come out of what remains of that horrid Orangevelt mine."

Clifford paused to consider the implications of what he was about to say. "Suppose I agree. How do you make money out of this? I mean, you had to buy the diamonds from someone. I buy them from you, presumably for more than you paid for them, and that generates some profit. Will that be enough to get you off my back?"

London, Three Years Earlier

"Your otherwise sound analysis assumes I paid full price for diamonds without documentation. That's unlikely to be the case. But the margins are – as you so cleverly point out – a sideline. The real value in this idea lies elsewhere."

"You're going to have to help me here."

"You've seen the long-term forecasts, right? Demand for diamonds will grow by double-digits for years to come, powered by the rapid development of India and China. But with no new mines being discovered, supply is expected to decline – quite dramatically after 2016. So there would be tremendous interest amongst the financial community in a new mine that's producing some very large stones."

The light finally went on for Clifford. "Or an old mine, bought for a song, that's now going gang-busters thanks to new management."

"Precisely."

"So the real money lies in an IPO."

"Ladies and gentlemen, we have a winner! Clearly your years at Delacroix didn't rot your brain quite as badly as I'd feared."

"Why are you doing this? I mean, I see your scheme could generate a lot of money. But it's also very high risk. Trading diamonds without Kimberley certs may not get you thrown in jail, but defrauding investors certainly would. You're a highly-paid and respected advisor to the Government of Botswana; why take the risk?"

For once Lithwick lost his aura of calm and self-control, which only proved to Clifford how close to the edge Lithwick had been the entire time. "Highly paid? *Highly paid*? Do you have any idea how much I'm worth?" He rapidly worked himself into a state of agitation. "Do the math: Botswana sells $3 billion worth of diamonds to Delacroix every year. If I can increase the price by just 1% –1%! – that's another $30 million in the government purse. No one else in government brings in anything close to that amount of money, not even the president. I make an exceptional contribution to this country; I deserve to be paid exceptionally well. But those bastards have me on a government salary, and keep telling me I should be pleased to earn what a minister gets even though I'm not a minister. Well, show me a minister who can do what I do. They're all vultures living off what I kill." By the end of his tirade Lithwick was shouting loud enough to make the phone vibrate.

Clifford sat in silence for a very long time, listening to Lithwick's hard breathing on the other end of the line. Finally he himself took a deep breath, made the sign of the cross, and jumped in with both feet. "I'm not sure there's much point in debating this. I really don't have any choice, do I?"

"Clifford, you ran out of choices at a little after 6 AM one week ago. Wrong place, wrong time I'm afraid."

"What happens next?"

"Would I be right in assuming you've told the chairman about our little encounter?"

Clifford stalled for time. "Why would I do that?"

London, Three Years Earlier

"Because we both know you're in well over your head, and from that vantage point calling in the corporate cavalry might seem like your only option."

"What makes you think I haven't called them?"

"The fact they haven't called me." Lithwick paused to think for a moment. "Or maybe you did call them, but they're not coming. Either way you're on your own."

Cornered, Clifford said nothing.

"Your silence speaks volumes. So, since your beloved employer won't help you, let me tell you what to do. Tomorrow you go to the office as usual. Ask to see the chairman right away; I think we both know he'll agree. Tell him you've decided to resign to protect the company's reputation."

"He won't believe you agreed to back off in exchange for my resignation."

"Of course not. That's why you're going to tell him the truth – or at least part of it. Tell him I'm backing your bid for Orangevelt, and that if our joint bid is accepted, I'll forget what I saw in the hallway."

"But you could just make a bid on your own. Why do you need me?"

"You're my front man. I can't buy a mine in South Africa without upsetting my employers in Botswana, and I certainly can't be seen doing business with the Devil Incarnate that is Delacroix. You can't buy a mine without my help. If we work together – with me in the shadows, of course – everyone wins."

"Will Weil buy it?"

"I'm nearly certain he will. If he thinks he's got some leverage on me, he won't worry about the leverage I've got on him. Mutually Assured Destruction is one of the best ways to ensure peace and harmony prevail."

"What if he points out I don't know a thing about running a diamond mine?"

"Remind him that Delacroix has let nearly 3,000 people go in the last three years, and that's your short-list of candidates to run the mine for you."

"You've really thought this whole thing out, haven't you?"

"Despite what you may have heard about me in the hallowed halls of #42, I'm actually a very good businessman. Stick with me, and we'll both make fortunes."

"If we don't get thrown in jail."

"Now, now. Time to get your game face on. You're about to resign from the world's leading diamond company!"

As Clifford hung up the phone, he found himself feeling – he could scarcely believe it - excited. His dream of returning to Africa to run his own company was about to come true. It would have been better, of course, if he'd managed to skip the part where he was blackmailed and agreed to commit fraud. But God works in mysterious ways, and maybe the horrors of the past week were simply the price he had to pay for becoming the rich and powerful man he'd always known he was destined to be.

CHAPTER 33

Gaborone, March 21, 6:50 a.m.

"Inspector? It's me, sir."

"So it is."

"How are you, sir? How's the weather?"

"The weather, Thomas? We have been through this already. It's hot. It's dry. It's Africa, dammit!"

"Oh. Yes, sir. Of course, sir. Um, I'm calling with news, sir."

"I am simply overjoyed to learn that the weather isn't the only reason for this call."

"Ah, yes, very droll, sir."

"The news, please, Thomas. The news."

"Right, sir. We've identified the victim."

"Which suggests you have a name you'll tell me in the 10 seconds or less it will take me to lose my patience and hang up this phone."

"William Sanford. 63. UK citizen. Retired. Spent 20 years in the Queen's Guards, and another 20 with the armaments division of Worthington Plc. Apparently a bit of a crack shot.

Liked to go hunting with the upper classes – private game reserves, that sort of thing."

"Worthington? That's interesting. I suppose it could be nothing more than a natural progression for someone with a military background. But it does make me wonder if there's an angle we're missing here. Does Worthington have any connections with Botswana?"

"No, sir. I checked." It was all McLean could do to keep from sputtering in surprise at Thomas's newly found initiative. "Never had a war. Being a landlocked country, they have no navy. I got that from Wikipedia, sir. It's a sort of encyclopedia on the Internet, and you can look up all sorts of…"

"Thomas! It may surprise you to know that I'm not completely ignorant of the modern world, and in fact know what Wikipedia is. Go on with your findings."

"Yes, sir. Of course, sir. I didn't mean to imply, sir, that you were…"

"Thomas!"

"Right, sir. Combined, the Army and Air Wings have only 9,000 soldiers. They spend more time fighting poachers than they do other countries."

"No border skirmishes or anything like that?"

"There is a problem with South Africans crossing the border in search of work. But when the guards catch someone they simply send them back."

"And the ones they don't catch? Do the locals blame them for every crime that takes place in Botswana?"

"I wouldn't know about that, sir, but it does stand to reason. However there doesn't seem to be a lot of crime. Breaking and entering and car-jacking have increased in recent years, as has the presence of armed gangs. But on the Foreign Office website the first travel risk listed is hitting wild animals on the road at night. Sounds bucolic, sir."

"So no crime related to diamonds?"

"Not that I've been able to find, sir. But I suppose that's because when it comes to diamonds, the bad guys are both outmanned and outgunned."

"Long may it stay that way, Thomas."

"Indeed, sir."

"Any record of this Sanford fellow going to Botswana for a game hunt? A man like that might want to try his hand at shooting lions or elephants."

"Botswana Immigration's records aren't great, but they can't find any evidence Sanford was ever in the country."

"Were you able to find *any* connection between the victim and Botswana?"

"Not one, sir. Neither of his employers had any business there. We don't have much information about friends and associates – he seems to have been a fairly private man – but so far we haven't uncovered anyone or anything that would tie him to the country."

"So let us assume for a moment Sanford had nothing to do with Botswana. That would suggest the REMEMBER GABORONE message was not his. Someone else must have used him – or just his body – as a messenger."

"Yes, sir."

"We can further assume that since the body was found in Delacroix headquarters, the message was intended for them."

"Yes, sir."

"And we can speculate there was at least one other person involved – even though the Delacroix security systems have no record of this – and it is this person who left the message in Sanford's pocket."

"Yes, sir."

"But we still don't have a clue who that person was, or what the message was intended to communicate."

"Yes, sir. I mean, no, sir. No we don't, sir."

"And that means we're where we've been all along: stuck at the starting gate."

Both men were silent for several minutes, lost in their own thoughts. It was Thomas who broke the impasse. "Sir, I told you that I confirmed Sanford had no connection with Botswana. But we haven't yet looked into whether he was linked with Delacroix."

McLean was struck silent by the quality of the observation. "Thomas, if you keep this up, someday you might be a policeman."

"Yes, sir."

"And don't stop with the direct connections. See if he was associated with anyone associated with the company – especially someone who left under duress."

"Why is that, sir?"

"We still don't know what REMEMBER GABORONE means, but given the state of the messenger we can assume whoever sent that message is not a fan of the folks at #42 Farringdon Road."

"How should I go about finding those people, sir?"

"Start in HR. Find out who's been fired in the past few years, or left under less than pleasant circumstances. See whether anyone has sued the company for wrongful dismissal. If you get desperate, ask them directly whether they can think of anyone who might want to harm the company or its reputation."

"And if they can't come up with any names?"

"Then they're lying, either to us or to themselves.

CHAPTER 34

London, Three Years Ago

"Julia, it's Clifford Watkins. Could you possibly find a 5-minute opening in the chairman's schedule? I'd like to update him on the conversation we had a few days ago."

"Hold on – he's just walking past. Let me ask him."

This time Clifford was expecting an audience at some point during the day, but even he was surprised when the chairman's secretary came back with, "He'll see you right away".

Clifford walked up the stairs and towards the corner office, feeling apprehensive but surprisingly excited about the strange turn his life was about to take. Maybe what had happened in Gaborone was a blessing in disguise. He was never going to get rich working for Delacroix; being an entrepreneur – with important friends in high places – promised to be both more lucrative and more satisfying.

"Clifford, please come in. Tea? Coffee?"

"A coffee would be lovely, thanks."

Once Julia had left the room and shut the door, the chairman said "You seem much more at peace than the last time we met. Does that mean you have good news?"

"I think it does, sir. I did as you suggested, and you were right: there is something Lithwick wants. You were also right about what it is. However his scheme for getting it is far more, um, ambitious than I had anticipated."

"Well, the key thing is you've found a solution. Well done!"

"Thank you, sir. Unfortunately that solution will require me to resign from the Firm, with immediate effect if that's acceptable to you."

The chairman leaned back in his chair, and absentmindedly stroked his prominent chin. His intelligent eyes were racing as his mind evaluated – almost instantaneously – all of the different ways he could play the hand he'd just been dealt. Having reached a decision, he folded his arms on his large mahogany desk, and looked Clifford straight in the eye.

"I see. Clifford, you're a fine young man and have given years of dedicated service to the company. We will certainly be sorry to see you go, but if you've made up your mind, it would be wrong for me to try to stop you. Instead let me wish you the very best in your new endeavors, and tell you that if I personally can ever be of any assistance to you in the future, please don't hesitate to let me know."

Clifford's jaw clamped shut. That bastard! Not only was the chairman leaving him to fight the battle on his own, he'd also blocked any possibility of being tainted by knowledge of the details. He'd managed to completely wipe his hands of the affair – Clifford cringed at his own choice of words – even though he had the most to lose. Clifford struggled to salvage even a tiny victory.

"I thought perhaps it might be best for all concerned if the company could give me some sort of severance package so I can keep body and soul together until something new comes up."

"I'm sorry, Clifford, but we're not currently offering an Early Retirement Program. And since it was your decision to leave rather than the company's, I don't think you would qualify for an ERP even if we had one."

Clifford realized he should have seen it coming. Delacroix had ruled the diamond world for over a century. They had done deals with despots, ridden out the fury over Apartheid South Africa and then neatly pivoted to being a very public supporter of the new black government. They had ridden the incredibly choppy waters of African politics, fended off endless legal attacks in the lawsuit-crazy USA, brought the Russians to heel, and escaped the clutches of the European Commission. You don't have a track record like that unless you're very clever, very agile, and ruthless beyond imagination.

"Can I at least expect a letter of recommendation?"

"Of course, Clifford. In fact, why don't I write you one myself? I don't usually do that sort of thing, but under the circumstances it seems appropriate."

You brilliant bastard, Clifford thought as he got up to leave. *If I ask my boss to write the recommendation, he'll ask why I'm leaving. This way Clever Clarence controls the communication, and our little secret goes out the door with me.*

Clifford took the stairs down to avoid seeing any of his soon-to-be former colleagues. And with each step his anger grew. *I gave up my career in order to protect the company, and in return I don't get a pound or even a penny. I get a goddamned letter saying I'm a fine young man or some such paternalistic crap that would mean nothing to a potential employer.*

Maybe I should march back into that oversized office and tell his majesty that I've had a rethink and decided the best thing would be to let the story come out. You know, honesty is the best policy, let the chips fall where they may – all that rot. That would get me a severance package pretty damn quick.

Sure, if the story did come out I wouldn't look all that good. But the almighty chairman would look a whole lot worse. And reporters are going to be a lot more interested in scurrilous gossip about one of the world's richest men than in anything I have said or done.

For that matter, why wait? Maybe I should leak the story. Not just in Botswana, but here in the UK. Plus all the trade papers. The Botswana Government would probably give me a passport and a pension in thanks for all the damage that would cause.

As he reached the ground floor, Clifford considered turning in his ID badge, and decided against it. *For better and for worse, Delacroix made me the man I am today.*

Tomorrow I become my own man, working as the public face of a bitter lunatic with a criminal business plan. What could possibly go wrong? And with that Clifford Watkins walked out of #42 Farringdon Road for the last time.

He didn't look back.

CHAPTER 35

Antwerp, March 5, 11 a.m.

At long last, it was done.

42 carats, G color, VVS2 clarity, Excellent cut. Every year about 90 million carats of diamond are cut and polished, yet less than a dozen stones are in the same league as the one sitting on Daniel's workbench. With oil prices high and Middle Eastern sheiks feeling flush, this single diamond should fetch over $3 million.

Of course, Daniel would never know for sure since this stone would never appear on the open market. No, Daniel was going to sell it to an intimidating Afrikaner who negotiated politely over the barrel of a gun. Daniel's best-case scenario was to establish $3 million as the market price, subtract the 30% discount Frans had insisted upon, and settle for $2.1 million.

Still, his disappointment went only so far: that was $600,000 more than he had paid for the rough. It was a huge profit for someone used to making a 7-12% margin on diamonds selling for $20,000 or less. So Daniel told himself to stop thinking about how much he could have made in an imaginary world where he bought the diamond at a discount but sold it for full price, and accept that things had actually turned out quite well here in the Land of Reality – a whole continent Daniel suddenly understood he'd never visited before. With that uplifting thought in mind, he called the number he had been given. It was answered on the first ring.

"Hello, Daniel." The voice reeked of false warmth.

"Your, um, order is ready."

"Excellent! What have you got for us?" In reply, Daniel described the diamond in considerable detail. He had just started to wax poetic about the stone's exceptional fire and brilliance, when the man asked him to hold the phone. A voice Daniel had never heard before joined the call.

"Daniel, hello. I haven't had the pleasure of meeting you in person, but Frans has been keeping me apprised of your progress – which I've followed with tremendous interest. And I must say I am very, very impressed with your work. 42 carat G VVS2 Excellent? That's several grades higher than even I had hoped for. Have you had the stone graded by GIA?"

"Just got the certificate this morning."

"Well, then it's official. By the way, did they ask you anything about the stone's provenance?"

Daniel considered lying, but lost his nerve. "No, they didn't."

"That's very good indeed, isn't it Frans?" Frans agreed that it was. "That means our discussion must now advance to the ever-difficult area of price. Have you given any thought as to what this wonderful diamond might be worth?"

"Well, I did a little checking of recent auction prices. There hasn't been anything too similar of late, but splitting the difference in price per carat for smaller and larger diamonds, I came up with... $75,000/carat."

"That's quite a bit higher than my own calculations. But let's say – for a moment, at least – that you're right. That works out to over $3 million."

"Given how rare a diamond of this size and quality is, $3 million sounds about right to me."

"I'm sure it sounds marvelous, but I lack confidence there are any buyers willing to sing the same tune. Shall we say $2 million?"

Daniel's immediate response was to grab the money and run. $2 million would leave him $500,000 ahead, and bring this rather scary chapter in his life to a happy and welcome end. But a *diamantaire* never, ever accepts a first bid. Doing so would send all the wrong messages: The initial asking price had been ridiculously high. The buyer's offer was more generous than it needed to be. The seller was a weak negotiator who could be pushed around in future transactions. That sort of thing could ruin him for life. So Daniel dug around in his gut until he found some nerve, and said "$2.5 million is as low as I can go".

"Daniel, friends should never be reduced to haggling. Let's split the difference: $2.25 million."

Unbelievable. The man had actually offered more than Daniel was willing to accept. Better say yes, but not too eagerly. "You're right. We shouldn't haggle. You gave me a good deal on the rough, so I'm willing to do the same on the polish. $2.25 million it is. *Mazal.*" As the Yiddish word with which even non-Jews close a diamond deal passed his lips, Daniel felt a huge surge of relief. At long last the nightmare seemed to be over. Achmed Khalif would get paid. Frans and his gun would disappear. Daniel Stern would have joined the ranks of men who have both cut and sold a Special. And he'd be $750,000 richer than when the whole thing started.

They agreed the pickup would be made in Daniel's office the following morning. Daniel thought about asking for an the exchange in the Bourse, where he would be surrounded by people who knew him – people who could come to his rescue if Frans went drastically off script. But Daniel's fear for his personal safety paled in comparison with his fear for his reputation – and thus his livelihood – if his colleagues discovered he was dealing in dirty diamonds.

At precisely 8 AM the following morning, Frans ignored the bell and banged on Daniel's door with his massive fist. Daniel answered as quickly as he could, hoping none of his neighbors had heard the pounding.

"Good morning, Daniel. I hope everything is in order?"

"It is. Please come this way; the diamond is downstairs in my work room."

Daniel was about to shut the door behind Frans, but then noticed he was not alone. Five huge men in black leather jackets were standing at the bottom of the stoop. Only two moved to cross the threshold; the other three turned their backs on Daniel, and formed a protective semi-circle around his door.

"Security, Daniel, nothing to worry about. When we transport a diamond as valuable as the one you've created, we want to make sure it reaches its destination intact."

Daniel didn't believe that for a minute, but it wasn't a bad lie to give the neighbors if necessary.

"Of course. I'm glad you're being careful. Please have a seat while I unlock the safe." Daniel had taken the precaution of dialing in all the numbers except the last, so there would be no possibility of Frans stealing the combination by watching him carefully while he twisted the dial. As the heavy door slid open, Daniel quickly grabbed the 42-carater, which he'd placed in a black velvet presentation box.

"Isn't it stunning?"

"You're asking the wrong man, Daniel. I can tell it's big, and therefore likely to be expensive. But my knowledge of diamonds ends there."

"So you're not going to inspect the stone to make sure it's what I said it is?"

"No need, Daniel. We trust you. And if we didn't, we know where you live." Frans smiled to indicate he was making a joke, but Daniel didn't find it the least bit funny.

"I see. Well, have you brought the money?"

"It will be wired to your account the second I walk out your door. You should be able to access the money by the end of the day."

"Ok, I'll have Brinks deliver the diamond wherever you'd like as soon as I can confirm the money is in my account."

"We'll be taking the diamond with us."

"What? How do I know you'll actually send me the money? You may know where I live, but I don't know the first thing about you."

"You're going to have to trust us, Daniel, on this and some other – what's the mot justes? – matters of mutual interest."

So there it was. Daniel had no cards to play, and everyone at the table knew it. All that was left to him now... was prayer.

"Of course. Let me just prepare the diamond for transport."

"Excellent. Now that our first... *cooperation* has gone so well, shall we talk about future possibilities?"

"Such as?"

"Do you have any experience working with diamonds from Zimbabwe?"

"Nobody does. They haven't been cleared for export by the Kimberley Process."

"Not yet. But they will be soon, at which point the prices will skyrocket. Better to get in now, while there are still bargains to be had. Don't you think so?"

Antwerp, March 5, 11 a.m.

"What exactly have you got in mind?"

"Maybe you should take partial payment for today's transaction in rough rather than cash. Say, $1.5MM worth of Zimbabwe diamonds in lieu of $1 million in cash?"

"If I were willing to trade in dirty diamonds I could get $1.5 million worth of Zim goods for $750,000. Everyone knows they're offering massive discounts to persuade *diamantaires* to ignore the Kimberley ban. At $1 million I'd be losing money."

"Quite the contrary. You'd be making an additional $500,000 once the stones are polished. And because you'd be dealing with us – people you *trust* – you wouldn't have to lie awake at night worrying about whether jumping the gun just a little bit was going to get you in trouble."

"I think I'd rather take the cash."

"Why don't you think again, Daniel, and let us know by lunch time. Meanwhile I'll have $1.25 million sent to your account." And with that, Frans turned to go. Daniel walked him to the door, said his goodbyes, and collapsed on the floor. It took him nearly 15 minutes to regain enough strength in his legs to climb up again, stand unsteadily for a few moments, walk over to the window and look out. What he saw nearly made his heart stop.

The three burly bodyguards were still there. Apparently they were going to help Daniel reach the right decision about the Zimbabwe diamonds. Daniel gingerly took a few more steps on his still trembling legs, dropped into a chair, and let his head fall into his hands. There was no longer even a shred of doubt: he had been expertly maneuvered to the darkest, most disreputable, and most brutal side of the diamond business. And he absolutely no idea how to find his way back.

CHAPTER 36

Gaborone, March 32, 6:05 p.m.

As McLean opened the door to his room from the hallway, he noticed a piece of paper had been slipped under the door:

Tonight Only!
Abena Kainyah
Live in Concert at the Grand Palm Resort & Casino Grand Ballroom
Doors Open at 7 PM
Good Seats Still Available

Abena Kainyah is Africa's best-known recording artist. With more than 15 albums to her credit, she is loved by fans everywhere – from her native Ghana, to Los Angeles, to London. She has performed with such top international stars as Alicia Keys, Tony Bennett, Carlos Santana, and Dave Mathews. Her style is rooted in African rhythms, but is influenced by R&B, Caribbean, soul, Cuban and reggae music. In addition to her musical success, Kainyah is known for having built more than 50 schools for girls throughout Africa.

McLean had never heard of Abena Kainyah, but that was scarcely surprising. As his wife was forever telling their friends, "Ian's view is there hadn't been a single decent song since the Beatles broke up." But when in Rome and all that. Plus, the alternative was spending yet another night looking at his case notes in the musty shoebox that was this room. Better to go and live like a local for one night. Besides, if it was loud and annoying, he could always walk out and head straight to the bar for a nightcap.

He called the concierge to arrange a ticket, and room service to arrange a quick burger and a Windhoek beer. All three came on time, and the burger and beer went down surprisingly well. Feeling somewhat proud of himself, he made the short walk over to the ballroom, arriving at one minute before 7 PM.

There wasn't another ticket holder in sight. "In for a penny, in for a pound" McLean said as he handed his ticket to the massive t-shirted guard at the entrance; the man obviously had no idea what McLean was talking about. He quickly found his seat, helped by the fact it was in the back. And then he waited.

By 7:30 the room started to fill up, but it was closer to 8 before the lights dimmed and the show began. Much to his surprise, McLean found himself swaying slightly as the rhythm of the base guitar worked its way into his soul. Then Kainyah came out, dressed simply in faded jeans and a black silk shirt, and the place went wild. She sang in English, French, Spanish, and several different tongues that McLean guessed were various African languages. Regardless of what language she was singing in, everyone in the crowd – except him, of course – knew all of the words. And most of them were on their feet, dancing as if the music had taken possession of their bodies. After a solid 20 minutes of non-stop rock 'n roll, Kainyah took things down a notch so she could speak to the audience, and the band – who had been sweating profusely from the very first drop of the beat – could replenish themselves with quickly-drained bottles of cold water.

"I'm so happy to be here in Botswana, and to share my music with all of you. You know, people often ask me how I got started singing, and I tell them I didn't. I got started dancing... when I was five years old. That's the first time I heard The Rolling Stones sing *Satisfaction*, and I just couldn't stop my body from moving. 'Oh, momma', I said, 'what is this music?' She said it's The Rolling Stones. I said 'where in Africa are they from?'" The crowd registered their amusement with a loud, collective laugh. "She said 'they're not – they're from England'. And I said, 'they have black people in England?' And my momma laughed. 'Child, those boys are as white as your nightdress.' I couldn't believe it!"

The audience roared.

"I learned something important that day. No matter who we are, or where we live, music is one thing we can all share. And my dream is that some day we will share all things – not just music, but food and education and clean water and safety – with people from all over the world. That's why I wrote this next song, which is called *Diamonds in the Dust*."

It was a slow but powerful song, with some extraordinarily lovely sustained harmonies. For once McLean found himself actually paying attention to the lyrics:

Along a hot dusty road
An old woman slowly walks
Looking for something, anything
For her family to eat.

She stares at the ground
Pushing the dirt with a stick
Hoping, hoping to find
A diamond in the dust.

Most days she finds nothing
And goes home in tears
Her family's hunger
Like a hole in her heart.

So the next day she walks
Along that same road
Hoping, hoping to find
A diamond in the dust.

It was a beautiful and haunting melody, and McLean couldn't get it out of his head. When the performance finally drew to a close – after two encores performed in response to riotous standing ovations – he bought a concert CD, telling himself it was a present for Edith. He took it back to his room, threw it into his laptop, and lay down on the bed to listen to the song one more time.

"Her family's hunger/Like a hole in her heart." He couldn't imagine what it would feel like to be that poor. And

Gaborone, March 32, 6:05 p.m.

that made him think of Sister Mary Catherine, standing at the front of his second grade classroom with a long ruler in her hand, pointing at old black and white photos of starving children, and warning her charges to remember that 'there but for the grace of God go I'.

It's easy to play by the rules if you have a roof over your head and food in your belly. But not everyone is so lucky. And for the less fortunate, exceptions have to be made. McLean and just about every cop he knew would turn a blind eye to a poor man stealing food for his family. But at what point did need become greed?

They say that behind every great fortune lies a great crime. McLean preferred the more actionable version of that idea that was drummed into his head every single day of his 6-month training period by a cynical old sergeant: *cherchez le bling* (he pronounced it "chair chay lou bling"). If you see signs of a sudden windfall – especially among a 'certain class of people' – you're looking at a crime. A tough guy who used to sit on street corners starts driving a fancy car? Pull him over; those wheels were probably stolen. Pat down a bad guy and feel a gold chain around his neck that hadn't been there last week? Check the pawn shops; odds are high it was traded for some of the jewelry stolen from that nice Mrs. Smith who got robbed last Tuesday. Greed: more often than not, that's how the bad guys got caught.

McLean bolted upright and turned as stiff as if he'd been hit by lightning. *Diamonds in the dirt.* "You idiot!" he shouted, even though there was no one to hear. "It was staring you in the face the entire time!" Slowly, the pieces began to fall into place, starting with the night Edith made him watch a documentary on the BBC about how armed soldiers, somewhere in southern Africa, were forcing children to mine diamonds. Most of the kids were standing in streams, like they were panning for gold. But the least fortunate were forced to climb down narrow tunnels that had been carved out of the mud. These makeshift mines were everywhere, and the reporter said that after every heavy rain hundreds of children were literally buried alive when the sides of those mines collapsed.

Beatings were common, and rapes a daily occurrence. While the soldiers all had flashy watches, designer sunglasses and other symbols of sudden wealth, the workers were literally starving to death. Several of the people interviewed for the program said the mining areas were little more than torture camps.

McLean had been outraged at the time, but his compassion and interest vanished the instant he turned off the TV. Now that he was in Africa, at the heart of global diamond mining, he realized there was more to the story than even the BBC had realized.

Getting the diamonds was only the first step; the stones were useless without a buyer. In the days before the Kimberley Process that was probably Delacroix, as their policy had been to dominate *all* sources of production in order to keep their monopoly intact. But once NGO's and global media started to highlight the horrors of blood diamonds, Delacroix decided the – McLean struggled for the right word -- *risks* associated with diamonds of uncertain provenance were far greater than the rewards. So from 2000 onwards, all Delacroix diamonds came from mines owned by the company.

Or so it said on their website. It was possible, McLean thought, that Delacroix was still buying dirty diamonds on the sly, and then mixing them in with legitimate goods. But the sheer size of the company made that difficult to pull off, since many people in multiple departments in various countries would have to be involved – and each one trusted to keep his or her mouth shut.

Another problem with the conspiracy theory: as the most dominant player in the industry by far, Delacroix was closely tracked by industry analysts. They were likely to have extensive data on what the various Delacroix mines were capable of producing. A sudden change in quantity or quality would surely be noticed.

A small company, on the other hand, might find it easier to mix dirty stones with clean ones. The authorities knew less about them, and paid them less attention. This relative lack of oversight would make it much easier for the unscrupulous to fly under the radar. With that thought bouncing around in his brain, McLean ejected the Kainyah CD, and eventually got a feeble connection to the Internet. He typed "diamond mining companies" into Google, and saw there were about a dozen. He eliminated Zandex and LRT, as both were divisions of very large public companies which would be doing the same risk:reward analysis as Delacroix. He also crossed off Northern Diamonds, which was effectively owned by the Canadian government. Next he eliminated two more companies that were so small the illegitimate goods would have stood out. That left him with just four solid possibilities:

1. Gem Mines International
2. Dia Monde
3. DiaMex
4. All-African Diamonds

Gem Mines had lost money for three straight years. If they'd had a secret windfall, they were hiding it well. Dia Monde was up for sale, which meant more scrutiny than a scam could withstand. DiaMex was a possibility, even though their annual results tended to move up and down within a fairly narrow band. But when he got to All-African Diamonds, McLean felt a quickening of the pulse. He knew he was onto something.

All-African was run by a man named Clifford Watkins. It was formed almost four years ago in order to purchase the Orangevelt mine from Delacroix, meaning there was at least one connection with #42 Farringdon Road. After three years of operation the company had launched an extremely successful IPO, which netted $1.5 billion for Mr. Watkins and his investors. An article in the *Financial Times* said the high initial share price "reflected All-African's proven ability to find large, high-value diamonds in what had been thought to be an end-of-life mine."

The article also said that Watkins had spent 13 years working for none other than Delacroix.

Cherchez le bling, indeed.

CHAPTER 37

KwaZulu-Natal Province, South Africa
March 21, 10:30 p.m.

Clarence settled back into his favorite armchair, comforted by the gentle crackling of the aged leather. He looked around the room, his favorite in the entire house. Here there were no pictures of him shaking hands with royalty, heads of state, or the latest Hollywood sensation; that sort of thing was for the public areas. The library was his and his alone: simple, masculine, and very African. The pictures on the wall were all from a time before he was born, the era in which Delacroix was one of the greatest monopolies the world had ever known.

There behind him was Jonathan Weil, his great-grandfather and the company's second managing director, shown standing outside the firm's first offices on Kimberley High Street. Clarence had never met him, but judging from the photo he was a resolute man, totally intolerant of failure.

Next to him there was a photo of Clarence's grandfather, Leonard. He ran the company for just 11 years before a debilitating stroke left him unable to speak. In his prime, however, he was a giant among men. Although the tale was possibly apocryphal, most South Africans believe that one sunny afternoon he walked into the prime minister's office and dictated the terms of a new mining contract. He then spun on his heels and left, without giving the head of state the chance to say a word.

There was his father, Max, a difficult man in a gallery of difficult men. He was brilliant, no doubt. But it often seemed to Clarence that his father cared more about the Delacroix bottom line than he did his own family. He was a distant man who sent Clarence off to boarding school when he was just 13. That first year at Harrow had been the hardest of Clarence's life, one that both toughened him and made him realize just how easily he could be broken. To this day Clarence wasn't sure whether he loved his father or hated him; his hard-won solution to the problem was to believe those were two sides of the same emotion.

During his years of exile in England, Clarence wanted nothing more than for it to be his turn to take the reins at Delacroix. He saw himself as being a kindler, gentler leader than his father had been – but just as successful. He daydreamed about being the sort of boss the men in the mines would be genuinely happy to see, a true man of the people. But these happy visions were often interrupted by terrifying nightmares. The storyline was different each time, but ultimately they were all a variation on the same theme: would he be up to the job? Would he be worthy of the men whose pictures looked down upon him now? Would he be another great Weil, or – God forbid – the one who destroyed what four previous generations had devoted their lives to building?

Many times during his 20-year tenure Clarence had sat in this very chair, drinking his favorite Royal Lochnagar

KwaZulu-Natal Province, South Africa March 21, 10:30 p.m.

Selected Reserve Scotch, and pondering his options. More often than not, he'd made the right decision. There was that day in 1996 when the European Commission – desperate for a high-profile scalp to justify its ever-growing budgets – announced its intention to break up the company. An 80% share of the world market for diamonds was proof Delacroix not only had monopoly power, but was abusing it. And the only apparent solution was to chop the company down to size.

Delacroix's lawyers proposed a complicated but clever strategy: they claimed that a monopoly in diamonds is a logical impossibility. After all, no one *needs* diamonds. So if consumers think the prices are too high, they can just stop buying them. That's very different from domination of – say – energy or transport services, which are essential to daily life.

Clarence did as he was told by the supposed experts, and made a speech on the theme at Stanford Business School – a fiasco he regretted to this day. As he mumbled the words "diamonds are different; diamonds don't *do* anything," he felt dirty and ashamed, unfaithful to both his heritage and the gem that had made everyone in his family billionaires many times over. On the flight home he could still hear the derisive laughter from the audience, an audience of *students*, no less. And what made the shame even worse was the fact they were absolutely right: it was a dumb argument to make.

The next morning he went into the London office, gathered his senior management team and the army of lawyers, and told them the strategy was going to change. No more debating at a philosophical level; regardless of whether that argument was logically right or wrong, it was a loser. There was simply no way the European Commission was going to publicly announce that they'd gotten it all wrong, and a monopoly in diamonds was o.k. by them. Delacroix was going to have to give them some small victories if they had a hope of winning the bigger battle.

The senior counsel began to argue the point, but Clarence silenced him with a raised hand. "The decision has been made," he said.

The executive team asked for details, and were told that Delacroix would end the sales agreements with both the Australians and the Canadians. "But that will cut our global share by more than one-third!" the director of sales blurted out.

"Yes," said a very calm Clarence, "it will."

"And it means we will have just over half of the world market."

"Yes," Clarence agreed again, "it does".

"This company has been built around effective control of the supply of diamonds. With a share of just 50%, that strategy becomes meaningless. Why we, we... we wouldn't have a strategy at all!"

The outrage continued for a good five minutes. Clients would be disappointed. Delacroix was making it impossible for them to fill their cutting factories. They would be forced to deal with less scrupulous suppliers, putting the reputation of the entire industry at risk. Clarence listened to it all with a slightly bemused expression, and then raised his hand for silence once more.

"Gentlemen, let us not lose sight of the facts. Fact #1: we cannot continue to do business as we have done. The European Commission has thrown down the gauntlet, and they aren't going to pick it back up again without some concession from us. Fact #2: we make virtually nothing from the sale of either Australian or Canadian goods. When we look at the true costs of handling someone else's diamonds, it's clearly a money loser."

The Chief Finance Officer shuffled in his chair as if he was about to speak, but Clarence made it impossible for him to do so. "Fact #3: most of our mines lose money. We keep them so someone else doesn't get them, but that's a very expensive game to play. Put it all together, and it's obvious that while what I'm suggesting will make us a smaller company, it will also make us far more profitable. And that, gentlemen, is what our shareholders want. You can take it from me – your largest shareholder."

Clarence then stood and left the room, but his stunned audience spent another four and a half hours venting steam. It had taken nearly three months before Weil got everyone on board, or at least on board enough to stop trying to undermine the new direction in public. And it took nearly five years before experts both inside and outside the company acknowledged that Clarence had, in fact, been right.

That boardroom showdown was probably his proudest moment, the time when he felt certain he belonged on the wall in this library, honored as yet another of the Weil greats.

The contrast with today couldn't be greater.

For Clarence knew he was staring at failure. His future held not a knighthood, but quite possibly a jail cell.

He wouldn't mind losing the money. He was fond of some of the things his huge wealth could buy: the extensive gardens, the private jet, the stable of thoroughbreds. But like most people who grow up rich, he actually had very simple tastes. He was quite content with a dinner of beans on toast while reading a good book in front of a roaring fire. In fact, given a choice between that and yet another interminable gala evening, he'd opt for the night in.

No, he was more concerned about losing control of the company his family had led for generations. If he were forced to resign, there was little chance the Board would accept his son as the next MD. Instead there would be calls for "new blood", which meant an outsider. And no matter how competent a manager he was, no matter how visionary a leader, he would never feel the same way about the company and its legacy as a Weil would. That was simply unacceptable.

Clarence thought he could weather the whispers about him having a gay affair. In England it was understood that at boarding school having another boy was not a perversion but often the only option. Experimenting with that sort of thing was not only accepted, it was practically expected. True, the incident in Botswana took place several decades after he'd gone down from Oxford, but while his wife might get some pitying looks, few in the upper classes would care. If anything, formally denying that anything had happened beyond a bad night's sleep and a hangover might make the incident seem far more important than it actually was. Best to say nothing and let the tabloids wear themselves out.

His professional behavior was a different story. When Clifford Watkins suddenly appeared with the funds and the desire to buy the Orangevelt mine, should he have disclosed their relationship -- however tenuous? Should he have recused himself from the decision to accept the bid? Should he have raised questions about how a junior employee who hadn't worked in months suddenly had the money to purchase a diamond mine? Clearly the man had financial backers; figuring out who and how wasn't Weil's job.

But that excuse didn't fly with what happened next. When the Orangevelt mine announced its first few major finds, Clarence knew something was wrong. His Exploration and Mining teams weren't infallible, but they weren't stupid, either. They had been in that mine for more than 50 years; there was simply no way they had so totally misunderstood its potential.

If he was to be honest with himself, Clarence had to admit the possibility Watkins was seeding the mine *had* crossed his mind. But suspicion and £3 will get you a cup of regular coffee at Starbucks. Without proof it would not only have been irresponsible to go public, it could have exposed the company to litigation. What's more, any responsibility Delacroix had for what went on in that mine ended the second it was sold.

Clarence Weil was far from foolish; he knew his arguments made him look bad. But they were shining examples of ethical behavior compared with his biggest problem. When Inspector McLean interviewed him, should he have confessed to having some idea what the REMEMBER GABORONE message *might* be referring to? Should he have made the more damning admission that he not only knew who the victim was, he'd actually gone shooting with the man and that detestable Charles Lithwick? Should he have spelled out the whole terrible story right then and there, on the off-chance it turned out to be relevant to the investigation?

In retrospect, Weil thought perhaps even he hadn't realized all the possible connections at the time. He was so stunned by the failure of the security system that he wasn't thinking clearly – much less creatively. Maybe it had been several days before he put all the pieces together, and now that he had he would let the police know.

Weil poured himself another Scotch, and drank it down in a single gulp. Then he looked up at the photos again. "What would you have me do, gentlemen?"

Unbidden, Shakespeare's words danced across his lips: *"He who steals my purse steals trash. But that filches from me my good name robs me of that which not enriches him, and makes me poor indeed."*

Clarence massaged his neck with both hands, giving any dissenting voices a chance to be heard. There weren't any. The Bard, as always, was right. The reputation of the Firm must come first. There would be no volunteering of information that might prove to have nothing to do with the case. If Clarence's worst fears were realized, he would deal with them when the time came. For now he would carry on, showing no signs of weakness. Just like four generations of Weils before him.

CHAPTER 38

Gaborone, March 22, 2:15 p.m.

"Hello, Inspector. It's me. Calling from London."

"Thomas, you might be surprised to learn I could probably have worked that out on my own, given sufficient time."

"Oh. Yes, certainly sir. Sorry sir. I'm calling to report in."

"Don't let me stop you."

"We spoke with Fordham and Diamond Couriers International. Both said that there's absolutely no way anything could have been put into one of their shipments without them noticing. The boxes are locked by Delacroix in Botswana, South Africa, Russia, Canada, or Namibia, and can only be opened by Delacroix in London."

McLean considered the new information. "What if the item wasn't put into the boxes, but rather delivered along with them?"

"I asked that, sir." Inspector McLean found himself both surprised and strangely proud. Was the imbecile not an imbecile after all? "Both companies said it is their strict policy not to deliver anything that isn't on the manifest. Fordham said the receptionist at one of their customers asked the delivery guy to hand-carry a letter to someone on the shipping dock, which was his next stop. She was cute, he thought it was a harmless request, and said sure. They fired him for it."

McLean said nothing. He was willing to bet the occasional sandwich or Coke got hand-carried amongst friends. But this case wasn't about a small item that could be carried in plain sight without attracting attention. It was about a corpse and a bucket of pig's blood, both of which were likely to raise an eyebrow or two.

Assuming there were any eyebrows around.

"What happens if there's no one there when the delivery guy arrives? Can he just drop off the package?"

"Not with diamonds, sir. I couldn't get too much information out of the Head of Security; he said he'd go to jail before divulging any information that might get into the wrong hands and – quote – 'put diamond security at risk'. But he did say that diamond transfers run like clockwork, and the people who matter all know where the diamonds are at every stage of the process. When they arrive at #42 Farringdon Road there's a – I wrote down his exact words – 'there's an highly experienced and heavily armed team waiting to welcome them'."

"So they didn't use the diamond delivery system. What about ordinary packages?"

"The company has an exclusive contract with Global Express. I spoke to a representative who said it only covers documents, not freight, and the largest item delivered to #42 in the last three years weighed less than 10 pounds."

"What about larger packages – computers, printers, stuff like that?"

"It goes to the mail room, where it's logged. The addressee then has to come down himself – no secretary stand-ins on this one -- sign for the package, and carry it out himself."

"So if all the systems worked as they're supposed to, it seems unlikely that the body could have been brought into the building by someone oblivious to what they were doing. And if that's indeed what happened, it can only mean one thing."

"Yes, sir. Inside job, sir."

"Either someone who currently works at Delacroix, or an ex-employee who still gets a free pass on some of the security procedures."

"The Director of Security swears that absolutely everyone – from the chairman on down – has to have the proper credentials or they don't get in."

"I'm sure that's the theory, but there's always someone who left his ID in his other pants. Or followed a co-worker out of the building for lunch – tailgating, the Americans call it – and didn't realize he'd left his ID at his desk until he tries to get back in. Whatever the policy is, I'm sure the reality is that occasionally a well-known face gets waved through."

"I completely agree, sir. But it's a lot harder to get waved through when you're carrying a corpse."

McLean choked back a laugh. Before he had a chance to think through the implications of breaking with tradition, he said "Good work, Thomas," and ended the conversation.

As he hung up the phone, McLean reflected on what he'd accomplished during his five days in Botswana. "That didn't take long," he said out loud. To be fair, he had learned quite a lot, but with the unfortunate side effect of closing off most of his leads. He was, sad to say, at a dead end. Still, he'd faced brick walls before, and eventually been able to knock most of them down. So he decided to apply the same technique in Botswana that he normally used at home.

He went out for a curry.

West Gate Mall was surprisingly upscale, and as he walked into the Chutney Restaurant the smell of Kerala-style lamb curry welcomed his nostrils like an old friend. The restaurant was packed, with a surprising number of Indians, and it was almost 20 minutes before he was seated. After ordering *dosa*, grilled prawns and the lamb, McLean got to work on the oddly named – but locally brewed – St. Louis beer the waiter had brought together with a nearly clean glass. It was a bit watery, worryingly close to that abomination Americans call "light beer", but if he drank enough of them they would undoubtedly find a way to get the job done.

Unlike McLean himself.

The chef sent over a plate of complementary *samosas* to help the beer go down. McLean eagerly bit into one, and promptly burnt his tongue. That reminded him of the old saying: bad luck is the only luck I've got.

Gaborone, March 22, 2:15 p.m.

Then again, he wasn't the only one. William Sanford was probably singing that as he died. Of a heart attack, not a gunshot wound. Was that just an unfortunate incident? Or did something – or someone – cause the heart attack? The autopsy found no trace of drugs that could have stopped the heart, and Sanford's medical records showed he was suffering from both clogged arteries and hypertension. So maybe his ticker just gave out at the wrong place and the wrong time.

But in that case, why shoot the poor guy? Judging from how little human blood was found at the scene, the coroner estimated Sanford had been dead for over an hour by the time he was shot. Forensics couldn't find any sign a gun had been fired inside #42. So the most likely scenario is the guy died of a massive heart attack, got shot an hour later, and then had his corpse dumped inside the most secure building in the UK without being seen. Made no sense at all.

Nor did anything else. A dead guy with a note saying REMEMBER GABORONE in his pocket. Except he's never been to Gaborone, or Botswana for that matter. Thomas had checked the records for Sanford's home and mobile phones, and not a single call had been placed to a number beginning with 257 – the dialing code for Botswana. So as far as it was possible to tell, the man who might have died so the world would Remember Gaborone knew nothing about Gaborone himself.

McLean nearly choked on his lamb. You idiot! Sanford didn't have anything to do with Gaborone *because he was simply the messenger*. Who was he carrying a message to?

Those nice people at #42 Farringdon Road. And God knows *they* have more than enough to do with Botswana.

But McLean's feeling of triumph quickly dissipated. There are easier ways to send a message than breaking into a heavily guarded building, dropping off a dead body, and pouring pig's blood around the scene for a touch of splatter movie excitement. Whoever thought *that* up wanted to attract as much notice as possible.

Any why make a public statement in a very private place?

Think! McLean could feel the answer was tantalizingly close, but just beyond his grasp. He scraped up the last of the curry with his butter *naan*, then froze with his hand halfway to his mouth. Marshall McLuhan! *The medium is the message.* The fake dead body and all the attention it attracted weren't meant to mislead the police. They were meant to tell someone in Delacroix – in the strongest, most frightening terms possible - "look how much attention I can attract if I decide to start talking about Gaborone".

There's a word for that sort of thing, McLean thought as he signaled for a third beer: blackmail.

CHAPTER 39

Johannesburg, March 6, 9:00 a.m.

"Hello, Clifford. How are you, my dear friend and business partner?"

"Well enough, Charles, given the circumstances."

"That doesn't sound good, now does it? Count your blessings, Clifford. You're young. You're rich. You own your own company. There are hundreds – thousands! – of people who would trade places with you in a heartbeat."

"Perhaps."

"Of course, being at the top of the food chain isn't always easy. No matter how much money you make for them, investors always want more. Am I right about that, Clifford?"

Suddenly Clifford found it difficult to breathe.

"Mining has its ups and downs. Everyone in the business knows that. But the investment community doesn't always see things that way. And no matter how many times you try to explain it to them, they either can't understand or refuse to do so."

"I don't know what you mean."

"I think you do, Clifford. I may not have the words exactly right, but isn't that a reasonable summary of what you told my associate the other day? You know my associate, right? Tall man. Blonde hair. Answers to 'Frans'. Any of this ringing any bells?"

"*You* sent him?"

"You make it sound like mailing a package. But yes, I asked him to pay you a visit."

"And you didn't think to mention that fact when I called you right after his visit?"

"The timing just didn't seem right."

"You asshole! That monster scared the shit out of me. I've been sleeping with a gun under my goddamned pillow ever since he left. And the whole time it was just you and your sick idea of how to send a message?"

"There's no need to use vulgarity, Clifford. I needed to send you a message, and judging from your reaction it appears I succeeded."

"What message? I've done exactly what we agreed. You knew we were going to use almost all of the large diamonds you had to pump up our prospects. You knew I would announce the IPO when our earnings peaked. You knew that – with only a handful of large stones left to find – our financial performance would decline, and that would bring the share price down with it. You told me you were going to sell out as soon as market enthusiasm started to wane, so you wouldn't be affected by the decline. I carried out my part of the agreement to the letter. If you didn't carry out yours, you have no one to blame but yourself."

"No, Clifford, I will *always* have you. That's the nice thing about our little arrangement – at least for me: you're the gift that just keeps giving."

"What in the hell is that supposed to mean?"

"It means, Clifford, that your next installment is due."

"Would you stop talking like you're some sort of oracle on the mountaintop, and tell me in plain English what it is you're expecting me to do?"

"With pleasure, Clifford! On Thursday Sotheby's is holding an auction of estate jewelry in London. You are going to go to that auction, and spend between $30 and $35 million on whatever tickles your fancy. And then you're going to put your purchases in a box, tie them up with a cute little ribbon, and give them to me."

"In exchange for what?"

"In exchange for keeping the fact you have committed massive fraud as our little secret."

"What? You're blackmailing me *again?*"

Lithwick laughed. "Yes, I'm afraid so. It's just so easy with you, Clifford. You have a rare gift for putting your foot into things, especially things that make me a lot of money."

"Say I agree to do this – and I haven't. Won't dropping so much money attract attention?"

"Almost certainly. But what difference does that make? You're a very rich man. You love diamonds, not least because of the wealth they've brought you. So it's perfectly understandable you'd take a small portion of your vast fortune to buy some superb examples of the miracle of nature that made you the man you are today. Come on, Clifford; you can spin that bullshit with the best of them."

"And if I do this, are we finished? Is it over between you and me?"

This time Lithwick's laugh was loud, long and genuine. "By my calculations you made close to $1.5 billion on an idea I created, funded, and executed to perfection. Do you really think a single payment of $30 million is fair compensation for my services? No, Clifford, you and I are going to be together for a very, very long time."

"And what if I refuse?"

"An anonymous tip is received by Interpol. You get arrested, and spend the rest of your life in jail. Your ill-begotten wealth is confiscated; they do that with the proceeds of a crime, you know. So you end up with nothing – except a lot of new friends who think you'd be an absolutely perfect sex slave. Or you can do things my way, continue to live in your lovely house in Johannesburg, keep your good name and about one-third of the money you made from the IPO, become a major figure on the auction scene – I know you like that sort of thing -- and continue wearing shirts from your Jermyn Street tailor rather than the unflattering horizontal stripes of a prison uniform."

Watkins picked up his water glass and hurled it against the wall. For some reason, the violence calmed him. "Not really much of a choice, is it?"

"Of course not. So when my trusted – though rather aged – assistant comes to visit you at your *pied-à-terre* in London on Saturday night the week after the auction, please welcome him with a smile on your face. His name is William Sanford, and he will see that your very thoughtful gift reaches me safely, with the minimum amount of interference from Customs, tax officials and other sorts of riff-raff."

"Is that it?"

"Except for one thing: Frans sends his undying love, and hopes to see you soon."

CHAPTER 40

Gaborone, March 22, 6:10 p.m.

"Good morning, Inspector. I hope I'm not interrupting your dinner."

"I'm impressed, Thomas. You've finally worked out this devilishly complicated time zone thing."

"Yes, sir. A couple of other things as well."

"You're on a roll. Let's hear what you've got."

"I asked Delacroix HR for a list of all the people who had been fired in the last 10 years. It was a surprisingly short list: just three names. I asked the woman in charge if she was sure it was complete, and she said – quote – 'we believe in choosing the right people and helping them acquire the right skills so that such extreme measures are unnecessary'."

"I wonder if the lady doth protest too much."

"I wondered the same thing, sir." McLean's jaw dropped; Thomas's transformation was becoming unnerving. "So I asked her for the names of everyone who had resigned as well. That was a much longer list, 27 names to be exact, not counting those who had been made redundant."

"Anyone of interest?"

"One from the first list, one from the second. Of the three guys who were fired, one set up his own company leasing diamond jewelry for weddings and other formal occasions. Apparently he's doing extremely well, so I figured he was unlikely to be holding a grudge."

"Sensible."

"The second guy moved to the Philippines and opened a beach bar on Bora Bora. I spoke with two of his former colleagues, and they say he's deliriously happy."

"So by process of elimination…"

"We have Charles Lithwick. He thought he was going to be the next Sales Director, and when he didn't get the job, he accused the guy who did of bribery. After he got fired he took Delacroix to court and lost."

"Probably not the company's biggest fan, then."

"Wait: it gets better. He's now part of the negotiations between Delacroix and Botswana over their new mining contract. And here's the shocking twist: he's on Botswana's side!"

"Bingo! Who have you got on the second list?"

"A man named Clifford Watkins. According to his former colleagues, he resigned suddenly after returning from a company conference. Everyone was surprised, as he'd never said a word about wanting to leave. And while the conference had its difficult moments, everyone I spoke to agreed it ended pretty well and that nothing happened that would cause Watkins to quit."

Gaborone, March 22, 6:10 p.m.

"Interesting, but no smoking gun."

"That's because I haven't told you the best part."

"Which is?"

"The location of the conference."

"Do I have to guess? Or will you eventually get around to telling me?"

"Sorry, sir. It was in Botswana. Gaborone to be exact."

McLean felt his heart beat just a little bit faster. "Ok. We've got a connection between Lithwick, Delacroix and Botswana. We've also got a connection between Watkins, Delacroix and Botswana. The first man clearly had – or has – a grudge. The second, well, we haven't got much on him at all. Any sign he was mad at the company?"

"Just the opposite. A few months after he left he bought the Orangevelt mine in South Africa from Delacroix. And that's notable for a couple of reasons. First, the guy had zero experience in mining. Second, none of his colleagues could figure out where he got the money. As far as they knew he was a middle class kid with enough money to pay the bills but certainly not enough to buy a diamond mine. Third, his was the only company to make a bid, suggesting all the experts thought the mine was worthless. Fourth – and this is the stunner – that 'worthless' mine started turning out very large diamonds – the kind worth tens of millions of dollars. On the back of those finds the company launched an IPO, and our Clifford Watkins was suddenly a rich man."

"How rich are we talking?"

"$1.5 *billion.*"

"Jesus H." McLean stopped momentarily to find his bearings in this flood of new information. "I agree all that sounds suspicious, but it doesn't sound like a reason to hate Delacroix. If anything, quite the reverse."

"I know, sir. I'll keep digging."

"Any connection between Watkins and Lithwick?"

"Not that we've been able to find."

"Damn. For one brief second there I thought we might be making progress." McLean could hear a sigh of disappointment coming loud and clear through the phone. "Sorry, Thomas. I didn't mean it that way. You've done some excellent work here."

McLean rang off, gathered up his notes, and headed to what had become "his chair" at the Kalahari Bar. In the grand tradition of Brits visiting the far reaches of The Empire, he ordered a gin and tonic. Then he spread out the case file, hoping a change in perspective would reveal something he'd previously overlooked. Two hours – and four drinks – later he gave up. Thomas's information was promising but a long way from proof. He'd need to talk to the two men himself.

Lithwick was presumably living in Botswana, so he'd be the closest. On the other hand, if he was working for the Botswana government, there was no way they'd let him be dragged before a British copper, with no jurisdiction, pursuing the slimmest of leads in a case involving the biggest employer in the country.

Gaborone, March 22, 6:10 p.m.

That left Watkins. Clifford Watkins. Where had he heard that name before? Thomas said he had purchased a diamond mine from Delacroix. That meant he should have been on the list of small mining companies he'd taken off the net after the Abena Kainyah concert. Where the hell is that damn list?

McLean started burrowing through his notes like a madman, causing two Chinese businessmen at the counter to look over at him in a blend of concern and annoyance.

There! There it was! And there *he* was. Clifford Watkins – CEO of All-African Diamonds! One of the companies whose extraordinarily rapid success raised questions about whether they were trading in blood diamonds.

Calm down, McLean, and get your thoughts in order. Breathe, man, breathe. Review what you know, calmly and carefully. Watkins worked for Delacroix, originally as a diamond buyer in southern Africa. When the company publicly stopped trading in conflict diamonds, he came back to London as an Account Executive. Had a perfectly normal career until he went to an executive leadership meeting in Gaborone in June of 2005. Came back and promptly resigned from the company. A few months later he makes an unexpected bid for an old Delacroix mine, even though no one can figure out where the money came from. The mine was supposedly tapped out, but in walks Watkins who finds one huge diamond after another, stoking market excitement. In 2008 the company has an IPO, and Watkins pockets $1.5 billion.

That's a lot of reasons *not* to be mad at the company. If anything, the evidence seems to be pointing at the reverse. Strange, though, that one seemingly ordinary guy suddenly has an incredible lucky streak. Finding the funding. Winning the bid for the mine. Stumbling on big diamonds Delacroix had said weren't there. Massively successful IPO. And it all happens following the meeting in Gaborone.

What the hell happened at that meeting?

Maybe Watkins had made some sort of secret deal with Delacroix? Why would Delacroix do such a thing? If the company wanted a business partner it could have done a lot better than a junior employee with no money and no experience in the field.

No money. Unbidden, the Abena Kainyah song *Diamonds in the Dust* started playing in his head again. He remembered the night of the concert, and how the song got him thinking about blood diamonds, which led to African diamonds, and now to Clifford Watkins.

McLean nearly choked on his drink. "I am a total and complete idiot", he said out loud. The two Chinese businessmen looked at him like he'd gone mad. McLean turned and addressed them directly. "I said, 'a total and complete idiot'. Enjoy your meal, gentlemen."

He immediately signaled for his bill, and then went upstairs to find a phone number for All-African Diamonds.

CHAPTER 41

London, March 13, 11:00 p.m.

Clifford didn't sleep for days. He'd lie down, completely exhausted, and close his eyes. But immediately ugly, frightening thoughts would force their way into his brain. Again and again he saw himself standing on the ledge of a very tall building, while from behind a voice kept telling him to jump. Some nights it got so bad he tried to imagine what it would feel like if he just let go, flying free through the air for a few wonderful seconds before his body was smashed to smithereens on the street below.

Again and again he tried to imagine a scenario that didn't end with him lying dead. Again and again, he failed. He couldn't tell the courier he was unable to buy the diamonds. His success at the London auction – and the inflated prices he'd paid – had been headline news in all the trade press and even in the *Style* section of the *New York Times*. He could claim he hadn't taken delivery of the goods yet, but that would buy him a couple of extra days at most – and what would he do with more time even if he had it? Maybe he should surreptitiously record the whole exchange, and threaten to take it to the police if they didn't leave him alone. It might work. Or it might invite a call from Frans and his 9mm Glock. Even if they didn't come after him, there was no way to tell the story without dragging himself down further and faster than Lithwick. All he'd really gain is some company out there on the ledge.

Finally Saturday arrived, and Clifford was still unable to come up with a plan of action other than doing exactly what he was told. He sat slumped over his small round kitchen table, drinking a cup of coffee he'd warmed in the microwave at least three times, each time forgetting to drink it before it cooled. I am well and truly screwed, he thought, and there's not a soul on the face of this earth who can help me.

Clifford froze. He could actually feel his brain shrug off its lethargy, and struggle to put together an original thought. He closed his eyes in hopes it would focus what little energy he had left on bringing this glimmer of an idea to life. And then, as if by divine intervention, he had it.

James Maxwell.

James was in his late 30's but still had the broad, rock-hard body of the rugby star he once was. He had grown up on a Yorkshire housing project, where – as he told the story to Clifford – his hobby had been getting into fights. It didn't matter whether he won or lost, although James usually triumphed. He just liked hitting and being hit; violence made him feel alive.

So did gambling. And that's how he and Clifford became friends.

James was one of the security guards at Delacroix assigned to accompany the shipments of diamonds in and out of #42 Farringdon Road. According to an extensive analysis

London, March 13, 11:00 p.m.

by the world's top security firm, the most dangerous time for a diamond delivery is those few minutes it takes to get the diamonds out of the truck and into their destination. The odds of getting robbed at this point are nearly six times higher than when the goods were in transit. So Delacroix put the biggest, toughest, most aggressive-looking guys onto delivery door duty, hoping to scare off anyone with criminal intent.

For two weeks out of every eight, James was very busy protecting the goods arriving for sale, and then being sent out to the clients who purchased them. But for the other six weeks of each sales cycle he was bored silly, and passed the time playing poker with whoever was available. Since the Account team was also on a Two Up Six Down schedule, many of them would nip down to the guard's break room to play a few hands, usually with a limit of just £1.

Over the course of several months Clifford got to know the guard about as well as one could over a game of cards. That changed one day when James was scooping up the pot after an unusually lucrative hand. "Guess it must be a birthday present from Lady Luck", he said. Clifford took that as a hint, and suggested they meet after work for a quick pint at the pub to celebrate the occasion. They stayed until the 11 PM closing time.

James's background was so different than his own that Clifford found him fascinating. And so every week or two he'd volunteer to stand another round of drinks, and the two unlikely friends headed off for evenings that usually ended with arms around each other's shoulders as they stumbled down the deserted streets of Smithfield singing at the top of their lungs. This went on for nearly six months before James suggested that tonight *he* would foot the bill.

Clifford found that a bit odd, but waited until they were well into the second pint before acknowledging the elephant in the room. "Something you want to talk about?"

"Actually, there is. But it's a bit embarrassing. I'm not the kind of guy who likes to ask his mates for help."

"That's what mates are for. Let's hear what you've got."

"Well, you know I like playing poker. And it's fun playing with the guys in the office, but with a £1 limit we might as well be playing gin rummy. So every once in a while I go to a private gaming house in Chinatown."

Clifford decided to help him out. "And you lost a bit more than you can afford."

"That's about the size of it."

"Does your wife know?"

"Nah, she'd bloody kill me."

"So how much do you need?"

"I'll pay you back, you know."

"It never occurred to me that you wouldn't. How much do you need?"

"£2,000."

"That's a fair number of bad hands. But it's not a problem. Cash, I assume?"

London, March 13, 11:00 p.m.

"Yeah, cash. Listen: that's not why I offered to buy the drinks. It's been weighing on my mind and I figured a few pints would help. I didn't mean to ask you to loan me the money."

"But you did, and I'm happy to help. Give me a few days to pull the money together. End of subject."

But it hadn't been. Eager to pay back Clifford as soon as possible, James had started gambling more rather than less. Within three months he owed Clifford close to £5,000, and it was apparent to both men that the debt was reaching the point it would be impossible to pay off on James's salary.

When Clifford left the company and moved to South Africa he lost touch with James, but he was certain the debt still bothered him, and would like nothing better than a chance to clear his account with his old friend Clifford. And Clifford really needed a large, scary man to sit next to him during the meeting with the courier.

So he gave his old gambling buddy a call.

CHAPTER 42

London, March 14, 5:00 p.m.

James arrived at Clifford's house an hour before the courier was scheduled to appear. Clifford had run though the entire scenario as simply, clearly and calmly as he could, but James still looked unsettled. "So they're sending over some geezer to pick up the diamonds?"

"That's what they said."

"Is he coming alone?"

"Supposedly. Said they don't want to attract attention."

"What do you need me to do?"

"Just sit there and look intimidating."

"What if he tries something on?"

"We'll just have to deal with that when and if it happens. But I think it's pretty unlikely unless I refuse to turn over the diamonds."

"Know who they're sending?"

"All they told me is that he's an elderly gentlemen. I would have thought that makes him a target for ordinary thieves, but I guess it's easier for an old guy to get through Customs without being searched."

"How bad are these people you're involved with?"

"I'm not really sure. They guy at the top is a nasty piece of work, but I don't think he's a physical threat. However he has hired muscle called Frans who I'll readily admit scares the crap out of me."

"Is the courier likely to be armed?"

"I wouldn't think so. If I can believe what they're telling me, this is just a normal business transaction between men of honor."

"Except you're handing over $32 million worth of diamonds and not getting a thing in return."

"True. I guess it's a somewhat unorthodox business transaction."

At that moment, the doorbell rang. Clifford looked through the peephole, and saw a man who matched Lithwick's description perfectly. 60's. Well-dressed to the point of debonair. Expensive haircut.

"Hello, I'm William Sanford. I believe you have a package for me?" Cut-glass accent. If he wasn't upper class, he was very, very good at faking it.

"Yes, of course. Please come in. I'll just get the package out of the safe."

Sanford came in, and stood obediently in the hallway with his hands folded across his body like a corpse. Then he saw James staring at him, menacingly. "I was under the impression it would just be the two of us, Clifford."

"James here is an old friend who just happened to drop by a few minutes before you showed up. Despite the perpetual scowl he's usually a pussycat. Don't let him unsettle you."

A few moments later Clifford returned carrying three jewelry boxes in a Tesco's shopping bag. "Please, sit down here in the living room so we can get this packaged up for you." Then, on a whim, Clifford decided to jump without a net.

"Do you have any idea what's in these boxes?"

"I was told it is a selection of estate jewelry."

"That's correct, as far as it goes. It's $32 million worth of diamond jewelry recently purchased at a Sotheby's auction."

"I see."

"Presumably you've been told to hand-carry it into South Africa, claiming these items have been in the family for years, and therefore aren't subject to duty or tax?"

"Switzerland, actually, and one of my lovelier female colleagues will pose as my wife, wearing two of the three pieces while claiming she wore the most expensive of the three at last night's charity ball."

"Very clever. Didn't you find it at least a little odd that you're not bringing me payment for these items?"

"I assumed that had already been taken care of, via a bank transfer or bearer bonds."

"That would be the case normally, but this is not a normal case. Would it surprise you to know I'm not getting a penny for any of this?" Clifford opened the jewelry boxes one by one to show off the stunning pieces sparkling inside.

"Very much so. But it's none of my business. I'm just the courier."

"How much do you know about your employer?"

"Just that he always pays promptly."

"Would it surprise you to know that he is a thief who trades in blood diamonds, is guilty of massive fraud, and is currently blackmailing me?"

Sanford's jaw dropped momentarily, but he quickly regained his composure. "I find that rather hard to believe."

"As well you might. But I assure you it's true. And while I'm the immediate victim, his real target is Delacroix. That means the instant you walk out of here with these diamonds in your possession, not only are you an accessory to a crime, you're also a direct threat to one of the most powerful corporations on the planet."

The elderly gentleman grew pale, and pulled out a handkerchief to wipe his suddenly sweaty forehead. "I had no idea."

"No reason you should have. But good luck convincing Delacroix of that, especially after James here returns to the company – did I mention he works security for Delacroix? -- and tells his superiors he's found the blackmailer."

"But I've got nothing to do with blackmail! I'm just picking up a package for a friend!"

London, March 14, 5:00 p.m.

"I'm certain the police will believe that someone you've never met just handed you $32 million worth of diamonds and didn't even ask for a receipt."

"This...this...this isn't fair. I'm completely innocent! I just got caught in the middle!"

"As did I. You see, your employer sold me some diamonds I thought were legitimate. Turns out they were blood diamonds smuggled out of places like Sierra Leone and the Congo. And for trading in those goods, I could go to jail. Like you I was a bit naïve, largely uninformed, and very likely to spend the rest of my life behind bars."

"I...I...I had no idea." Sanford swallowed hard, but it did nothing to bring color back to his suddenly sallow complexion. "Pardon me, could I trouble you for a glass of water? I suddenly don't feel very well."

Without saying a word, Clifford got up and went to the kitchen. James followed. "Think you're laying it on a bit thick?"

"Perhaps. But it's working. The old man is so terrified he'll agree to whatever we ask."

"How much of that stuff you're saying is true?"

"Very little, James. But I am being blackmailed."

"So what's the plan from here?"

"We go back in, and give Sanford both the diamonds and a message. Tell him to tell Lithwick that Delacroix sent a representative to the meeting, and they made it clear these pieces were to be accepted as payment in full. Any future attempts at extortion would result in 'extreme measures' being taken."

"You think a phony threat from Delacroix will put an end to all this?"

"It's hard to predict what Lithwick will do. But I'm almost certain he'll need to find another messenger. You saw how ill Sanford looked."

With that Clifford filled a glass with tap water, and returned to the living room – talking while he walked.

"You see, that nice Mr. Lithwick isn't so nice after all. In fact he's one of the most devious men I've ever met. And if you're not careful, he'll trap you in his spider web, just as he trapped me. I would advise you to rethink whether you wish to continue your role in this little operation, Mr. Sanford."

There was no reply.

"Mr. Sanford? Mr. Sanford, are you all right?" Clifford went over and shook the man, gently at first and then rather violently. "James, get over here. Check his pulse!" James lay two of his large, sausage-like fingers below Stanford's right ear, and waited nearly a full minute. Then he shook his head ever so slightly.

"He's dead? In my goddamn living room? Now what do I do?"

"Call 911."

"You think they can shock his heart back into action or something?"

"Clifford, he's gone. All they can do is take away the body."

"Jesus H. Christ. How the hell did I end up like this? None of this would have ever happened if Clarence Fucking Weil hadn't been such a damn coward."

"What does Weil have to do with this?"

"It's a very long story. And the moral is that guy doesn't care about anything or anyone but himself."

"You didn't say anything about Weil when you asked me to come over tonight."

"Well if this son of a bitch hadn't died on me, it wouldn't have mattered."

James began clenching and unclenching his fists, his anger looking for somewhere to go. "This is a pretty deep hole you've got yourself in."

"Don't you think I know that?"

"So what's the plan? How much of this story do you plan to tell the cops?"

Unbidden, an idea popped into Clifford's head and demanded attention. For the first time since Frans had appeared in his Johannesburg office, Clifford could feel the fog being lifted from his brain. He could see the outlines of a plan far more complicated, more difficult, and more risky than anything he had ever contemplated before. If it worked, Clifford would be free of Lithwick and Weil would get a message he would never forget. If it didn't, he'd end up in jail – but that was the ending to every other scenario he'd considered since Frans stopped by to say hello. Without saying another word to James, he ran to the hall linen cabinet and pulled out a blanket. He gently covered the body of William Sanford, feeling a moment of pity for a man who wandered into a drama where he knew none of the lines.

And his moment in the spotlight was just about to begin.

"James," Clifford said, "I'm going to need your help. And a gun."

"What?"

"I said I need your help. And a gun."

"Why the hell do you need a gun?"

"I'm going to shoot someone. But I need to do it quickly, before I lose my nerve."

"What makes you think I've even got a gun?"

"Do you?"

James dropped his head into his hands, and then looked up – staring Clifford in the eye. "Yeah. I do. But that doesn't mean I'm going to let you use it to do something stupid."

"I'm not going to kill anyone. I'm just going to shoot someone who's already dead."

"That sounds pretty stupid to me."

"May I remind you that you owe me a not insubstantial amount of money? Do this for me and we'll call it even."

"You said that when you asked me to come here tonight."

"And then we both got an unpleasant surprise." Clifford paused for a moment. "I wonder what Delacroix would think about a security guard with a gambling problem. Wouldn't they worry that creates an opportunity for blackmail?"

James looked at Clifford with a volatile mixture of surprise and disgust. "You really are a bastard, aren't you? And all this time I thought we were mates."

That one landed. Clifford's shoulders relaxed, as if someone had let the air out of him. "We are. And believe me: when I asked you to come here tonight I had no idea this was how it was going to go. But now I've got a dead body in my living room, a blackmailer robbing me blind, and not a whole lot of choices. I need your help, James."

The guard thought for a bit. "Why not make up a story? You know, say you're thinking of selling the flat and this guy came over to have a look. And then he died before you had a chance to ask his name."

"It might work – except for the fact there's no For Sale sign out front."

"Then say he was trying to sell you something."

"And I invited him into my living room instead of slamming the door in his face? No one would ever believe that. Besides, he's hardly dressed like a door-to-door salesman."

"Ok, ok. Lemme think. What if you say he came to buy some diamonds? You know, the ones there in the bag?"

"That might explain the body. But strange as it sounds, that's the least of my problems. Even if the police believe my story, I'm just buying time until Lithwick sends another messenger. And I'm unlikely to get this lucky twice."

"Lucky?"

"You know what I mean. My real problem isn't the dead guy; it's Lithwick."

"So turn him in."

Clifford turned away from his friend. "Let's just say I'm not completely without blame for the situation in which I find myself."

"How is shooting Sanford going to help?"

"You let me worry about that. Just get me the gun, and help get me into #42."

"#42? Why do you need to go there?"

"I need to send a message to Mr. Weil."

James's eyes bulged. "Wait a minute: You're not thinking of carrying a corpse into head office, are you?"

"The less you know, the less you need worry about."

"How in the hell will that help you with Lithwick?"

"Let's just say that Weil is as much a player in all this as I am. And if anyone can get Lithwick to back off, it's Clarence." Clifford said the name with so much hate resonating through his voice that even James felt afraid.

"Look, I won't pretend to understand the shit you've got yourself into. But one thing I do know is the security system at #42. And there's just no way you're going to sneak inside with a dead body, and get out with no one seeing you. The system is too good for that. It's foolproof."

"Not completely."

"Clifford, have you gone mad?"

"No, I don't think so. In fact, for the first time in a very long time I feel almost at peace."

"Jesus! You've really lost it."

"Perhaps. But now it's time to find out."

"How do you expect to pull this off?"

"Let me worry about that. All I need you to do is open the door for me."

"The guys in the monitoring room will see you coming in."

"I've got it covered. Just go to the office, hand me your ID card, and let the door close slowly behind you. I'll take care of the rest."

"Why do you have to shoot the guy? He's already dead, for God's sake."

"A guy who died of natural causes lying unnoticed on the floor is a security breach. I want to send a message."

"And just what is that message?"

"Back the fuck off and leave me alone. I'm tired of being manipulated. I'm tired of being used by both Weil and Lithwick. I tried doing it their way; all it got me was a lunatic Afrikaner with a gun in his waistband trying to make me wet my pants, and the greediest bastard on the face of the earth demanding I just hand him tens of millions of dollars whenever he asks for it. No more. I'm done with the whole damn thing. As soon as the dust settles I'm selling my shares and going into a well-earned retirement."

"What about me?"

"James, if you get me through this, I can promise you your days of working for Delacroix are over. I'll set you up for life, wherever you want. Surely your wife has had enough of London winters. Wouldn't she prefer a retirement home on the beach in Mozambique?"

James looked at Clifford, and then down at Sanford's lifeless body. Shaking his head, he left to get his gun.

CHAPTER 43

Johannesburg, May 23, 9:30 a.m.

"If you'd like to have a seat, Inspector, Mr. Watkins will be with you shortly. Can I get you a coffee or tea while you wait?"

"Tea would be lovely, thank you."

"English Breakfast or Rooibus?"

"English Breakfast, please. I have yet to develop a taste for the local brew."

McLean looked around the room. Everything was clean, modern, simple to the point of being stark – more like Scandinavia than South Africa. And not a thing out of place. Watkins was clearly a man who liked neatness and order.

"Good morning, Inspector, I'm sorry to keep you waiting."

"Not at all. Thank you for seeing me on such short notice."

"I'm always happy to help Her Majesty's government. I hope you won't think me impolite, but could I possibly see some identification?"

McLean was amused by the request, but nonetheless produced his badge and warrant card – which Clifford studied carefully.

"Thank you. You wouldn't believe how many scam artists we have in this country; one can never be too careful."

"Totally understandable. I realize a man in your position has a very tight schedule, so perhaps we can get down to business?"

"Certainly. And what business might I have with Scotland Yard?"

"Mr. Watkins, with all due respect, this will go more smoothly if I ask the questions."

"Of course. Forgive me."

"What is the nature of your relationship with Clarence Weil?"

Clifford tried to hide his surprise. He thought the interview would be about his purchases at Sotheby's or maybe the company's flagging share price. The question about the chairman of Delacroix landed a little too close for comfort. "I worked for him. Well, not directly, but I was with Delacroix for 13 years, ending up as Deputy Director of Sales."

"And during that time did you meet with Mr. Weil?

"Of course. We all did. The chairman was very involved with the sales side of the business. He inspected the goods before each sight – the sales events we hold every eight weeks – and signed off on the final allocation by client."

"In the course of that involvement did you ever have the opportunity to speak with Mr. Weil on a more personal level?"

"Yes. Again, we all did. Despite being one of the world's richest men, Mr. Weil is very down-too-earth and approachable."

McLean made a note. "Would you say your relationship with him was the same, less close or more close than your colleagues in similar positions?"

"I'm not sure I can comment on other people's relationships. But I always felt that Mr. Weil's door was open to me." As soon as the words were out of his mouth, Clifford heard the Freudian slip. It was all he could do to keep from giggling.

"Mr. Watkins, did you attend the Future Vision Conference in Gaborone in June 2005?"

That question held nothing to laugh at. In less than a minute, McLean had tied him to both Weil and the ill-fated conference in Botswana. Maybe the Inspector was on a fishing expedition, and still didn't know what linked those pieces of the puzzle together. But either he had his suspicions… or he was a damn good guesser.

Clifford tried to buy some time by faking a cough. "Sorry – I seem to have picked up a little something in London. What was your question again? Oh, the Future Vision Conference. Yes, I was there. As were all the top 250 executives in the company worldwide."

"Could you give me a brief summary of what took place at that conference?"

"It was supposed to be about the future of the company, as implied by the title. But we'd recently gotten the results of an Employee Engagement Survey, and they were shocking. So on Day 2 the agenda was thrown out and we spent the better part of two full days clearing the air."

McLean noticed that as soon as he asked about the contents of the conference, Watkins relaxed. Whatever happened in Gaborone that was worth remembering, it wasn't on the meeting agenda. "Would it be fair, then, to describe it as a somewhat dramatic – but otherwise fairly normal – company conference?"

"Yes, you could say that."

"So why did you resign from the company immediately after returning to London?"

"I had been thinking about resigning for some time. You've clearly done some checking on me" – McLean made no response – "so you know I started out buying diamonds for the company in southern Africa. I really loved that job: the travel, the excitement, the sense of being in control of my own destiny. But when the decision was made to exit that business and put the buyers to work as Account Executives in London, I lost interest. I'm just not cut out to be a tiny cog in the well-oiled machine that is Delacroix London. The Conference just confirmed my feeling it was time for me to move on."

"Did you discuss your decision with any of your friends or colleagues?

"No."

"Why not?"

Johannesburg, May 23, 9:30 a.m.

"I thought they might try to talk me out of it. And my heart was set on returning to Africa."

"Let's talk about that. Do you have any experience in mining?"

"I do now, of course, but you're right: at that point I was a novice."

"Is it common for people without mining experience to invest millions of dollars in a mine?"

"What I had, Inspector, was Delacroix experience. I know how the company works, what their overheads are. I know how much money they give away in order to appease governments in southern Africa who see them as a soft target. I know that a small company without all that baggage could make money where Delacroix had failed to. And I know diamonds. All I was lacking was the financial backing to put my plan into action."

McLean had to admit that sounded fairly plausible – except for one thing. "I wouldn't have thought there are too many people willing to invest in a mine run by someone without mining experience."

"And yet I found enough to make the winning bid."

"We'll come back to that. For now let's continue the story. Did anyone else bid for the mine?"

"No."

"Isn't that unusual?"

"I'm not sure you can talk about what's usual when it comes to buying mines from Delacroix. Until a few years ago, they never sold any."

"Fair point. So you buy this old mine no one else wanted, a mine that most experts said had nothing left but very small stones. And you find not one, but quite a large number of truly huge rough diamonds. How did that happen?"

"You'll have to ask Mother Nature, Inspector. Despite what I say in our analyst calls, diamond mining is as much luck as skill."

McLean pretended to check his notes. "Mr. Watkins, if someone were to bring you a large rough diamond, could you tell which mine it had come from?"

Clifford felt the hairs on the back of his neck rise. "Which mine? No. There's no one in the world who can do that."

"What about *country* of origin?"

"That depends. Diamonds from certain locations have a distinctive appearance. For example, diamonds from Zimbabwe are often coated with a sort of green film."

"What about diamonds from Sierra Leone and the Congo?"

"Those would be hard to identify," Clifford said carefully.

"Could you explain the term 'seeding a mine'?"

It was over. He *knew*. Maybe not everything, but enough to bring the whole thing crashing down on Clifford's head.

Better to come clean? Or try to skate across thin ice for as long as possible?

"It refers to taking diamonds from one mine and putting them in another."

"Why would anyone do that?"

"I suppose that depends on the person doing it. Perhaps he wanted to improve the output figures for a particular mine."

"In order to bump up a share price, perhaps?"

"Criminal motivations are more your area of expertise than mine."

"Mr. Watkins, if you wanted to buy a blood diamond, could you do it?"

"I don't know if I could, but I definitely would *not*. That's prohibited by the Kimberley Convention, and it's completely immoral."

"But you said earlier it's very difficult to identify where a particular diamond came from. So is it at least theoretically possible that you bought a blood diamond without knowing it?"

"Why would I do that, Inspector? I own a diamond mine."

"Just so. Let's go back to the Conference for a minute. We've spoken to a number of people who say you had a long conversation with the chairman over dinner on the second night."

"So? As I said earlier, he's a very approachable man."

"What did you talk about?"

"I don't remember. That was six or seven years ago."

"Did you happen to talk about your desire to buy Orangevelt?"

"I don't think so. At that point it was still more of a dream than a plan."

"Did you talk about conflict diamonds?"

"No, of course not. Why would we talk about that?"

McLean shrugged. "It's a major issue facing your industry and your company. I would have thought that's the sort of thing one *would* discuss at a Future Vision Conference."

Clifford's smile returned. "Perhaps during the working sessions, but over dinner our conversations are far more mundane. Cricket and football, mostly."

"I see. And what happened after dinner was over?"

"The chairman and I continued to talk for a while, and then we both went to bed."

"Separately?"

"Of course!"

"So you spent the entire night in your own room?"

"Yes! What are you implying?"

"Nothing. I'm just trying to clarify what happened that night."

Johannesburg, May 23, 9:30 a.m.

Clifford had a moment of panic. Had the housekeeping staff told someone his room hadn't been slept in? He should have messed up the sheets, but he'd been too unsettled by his hallway encounter with Lithwick to think clearly. *Christ, how much does this guy know?*

"Inspector, it was a long time ago. I can't be expected to remember every detail. And if you've talked to some of the other people who were there, you'll know it was a very emotional session. I think we all left Gaborone feeling like we'd been hit by a truck."

"And yet you were the only person who – immediately upon returning to London – resigned from the company. You had been there, what, 13 years by that point?"

Clifford nodded.

McLean again shifted gears, hoping to catch Watkins off balance. "You mentioned you worked as a buyer for Delacroix for a very long time. Would I be right in thinking that some times that work took you to countries currently prohibited from dealing in diamonds?"

"What are you implying?"

"I'm just trying to confirm a few things, starting with whether you have experience buying diamonds in countries that are currently banned by the Kimberley Process from selling on the open market."

"Yes, Inspector, I do. But if you're suggesting I used that time to trade for my own account, you're wrong. I was just out of university then. Where would I get the money to buy diamonds on my own?"

"Perhaps from the same backers who supported your purchase of Orangevelt."

"I didn't even know most of them until I presented my business plan for the mine."

"Do you know Thomas Sanford?"

"Who?"

McLean noticed with concern that Watkins appeared unfazed by the deliberately abrupt changes in his line of questioning, an old technique designed to unsettle even the innocent. The fact it didn't work on Clifford meant the man was quick on his feet. Tripping him up wouldn't be easy.

"Do you own a gun?"

"Yes. I keep it in the drawer of my night table, just in case. Unfortunately Johannesburg can be a very dangerous place."

"And in the UK? Do you own a gun there?"

"No, sir, I do not."

"According to Mr. Weil's appointment book, you had two meetings with him just prior to submitting your resignation. What did you talk about?"

"I told him I was leaving."

"On both occasions?"

"Yes. The first time I told him what I was planning to do. He asked me to reconsider. The second meeting was to tell him that I'd thought about it as he asked me to, but was still determined to resign."

"And that's all you discussed?"

"Yes."

"His secretary's appointment book notes the first meeting was in reference to – quote – "output from the Future Vision conference"."

"Just like I told you. It was the conference that made me decide to quit."

"She also showed us a glowing letter of recommendation the chairman wrote for you."

"Yes, he was kind enough to do so."

"However she was unable to recall any other instance in which the chairman wrote a reference letter for someone at your level. Don't you find that a bit strange?"

"Actually, I find it rather flattering."

McLean was nearly as impressed as he was frustrated. Watkins was not an easy man to catch. "I assume you heard about the recent incident at #42 Farringdon Road."

"The murder? Yes. It was a tremendous shock. Have you got any suspects?"

"Mr. Watkins, I'm going to share a little secret with you. There was no murder. Turns out the victim died of natural causes. And someone went to a lot of trouble to make us think it was, as you said, a murder."

"How remarkable! Why would anyone do that?"

"I think the more interesting question is *how*. Clearly it would need to be someone who knew the building and its security systems intimately."

"So you're focusing on the guards?"

"Oh, we're not thinking it's a guard."

"Really? I would have thought they'd be at the top of your list."

McLean shrugged. "One or more of them may have provided some help. But it's hard to see what their motive would be, especially given the clue."

"What clue?"

"It's something else we have not released to the press. You know, often the police withhold certain details of a crime, so that when they find someone who knows that detail they can be sure he did it. In this case, that clue was a piece of paper in the pocket of the deceased saying REMEMBER GABORONE."

"If this is supposed to be a secret, why are you telling me?"

McLean had to suppress a small smile of admiration: Watkins was good at this. But the Inspector knew that confidence leads to overconfidence, and that leads to sloppiness. He decided it was time to give Watkins a few easy ones that might cause him to lower his guard.

"Mr. Watkins, I'd like to go back to diamonds for a minute. Can you tell me about blood diamonds, the Kimberley Process, and whether the latter put an end to the former?"

Johannesburg, May 23, 9:30 a.m.

"Of course." Clifford gathered himself, like a self-important university professor preparing to enlighten a first-year student. "It's essential to remember that post-colonial Africa has been the scene of almost non-stop fighting. In Zimbabwe. Liberia. Sierra Leone. The Congo. Rwanda. The list goes on and on. In most cases the battles were between the government – legitimate or otherwise – and rebel groups. Governments usually have ways of financing their arms purchases, but rebels need to make money before they can make war. They naturally gravitate to whatever is easiest to steal. In a place like Rwanda it was foreign aid. In Nigeria, oil. In the Côte d'Ivoire, or The Ivory Coast, it was cacao. But in most of southern Africa it was diamonds."

Clifford paused to take a sip of sparkling water before continuing. "Diamonds are the most concentrated form of wealth known to man. That makes them easy to transport, and easy to smuggle across borders. They can be sold anywhere in the world, and once polished they're impossible to trace. For many rebel groups they were the perfect source of funding."

"How did the rebels get the diamonds?"

"In some cases they took over the mines. But most governments ensured the mines were well-protected, surrounding them with soldiers. For the rebels, it was far easier to go to the places where there are alluvials – diamonds found in or near rivers and oceans – and set up a perimeter guard. They let the citizens do all the dangerous work of digging and panning, then swooped in to commandeer the stones the second they were found. Anyone who didn't give the rebels what they wanted got shot on the spot, often in front of their families."

"Why did anyone go to the diamond fields in the first place?"

"They had no choice. The solders would enter a village, rape the women, shoot a few children to show they were serious, and tell the men they could either start mining for diamonds or have a choice of 'sleeves'."

"'Sleeves'?"

"Long-sleeves meant they'd cut off your hand at the wrist. Short-sleeves meant cutting off at the elbow."

McLean thought he'd heard pretty much everything during his years on the force. But this was an almost unimaginable level of brutality.

"Don't act so shocked, Inspector. It wasn't the rebels who came up with this idea. When King Leopold of Belgium was raping the Congo and stealing all its natural resources under the guise of colonialism, it was his troops who started the practice of cutting off the hands of the unwilling. They even sent the severed limbs back to Brussels as proof they were taking a hard line with the natives."

"So what happens once the rebels have the diamonds?"

"They find someone to buy them. Before the Kimberley Process came into being, that was almost inevitably Delacroix. But now it's mostly Lebanese traders, with the occasional Indian diamond dealer thrown in."

Johannesburg, May 23, 9:30 a.m.

"How do *they* sell diamonds without a Kimberley Certificate?"

"It's not nearly as hard as you might think. Fake certificates are readily available, though I'm told they're fairly easy to spot. As in all industries, there are unscrupulous people willing to turn a blind eye. And as far as I know, no individual has ever been prosecuted for violating the Kimberley Process. It's more about controlling countries than individuals."

"What's to stop someone from mixing uncertified goods with legitimate diamonds, and claiming the whole lot came from a compliant country?"

"I'm certain it happens. If you look at the published data there are countries that export more diamonds than they mine. Clearly they've got – shall we say – other sources of supply."

"But that's countries. What about individuals who want to skirt the rules? How hard would it be for them to mix clean and dirty diamonds?"

There it was: the ice cracking beneath his feet. But by now Clifford was skating so fast it was impossible to stop. "I suppose that depends on how aggressive they are. If they're adding small amounts of uncertified stones, and the individuals involved keep quiet, they would probably be very hard to catch. But as I mentioned a minute ago, if they get too aggressive the data will start throwing up red flags."

"So is it easier to pull this off with large stones or small ones?"

Clifford would have sworn McLean was smiling as he asked the question. "I really wouldn't know, Inspector. You'd have to ask someone who's actually done that sort of thing."

CHAPTER 44

Johannesburg, March 23, 9:47 a.m.

McLean once calculated he had conducted more than 6,000 suspect interviews, and he prided himself on his ability to read the temperature in the room. He was absolutely certain that Clifford had just gone cold – which meant the question about laundering large stones had hit home. Time to press his advantage. "We found the wheel prints, you know."

"What wheel prints?"

"The prints from the trolley used to transport the body to the second floor of #42 Farringdon Road. It wasn't easy: there were a lot of wheel trails on that carpet. But they all looked pretty much the same, the only difference being the depth – which of course reflects the weight of the load."

This was a bald-faced lie. Before tripping over Sanford's body, the unfortunate Maria had already vacuumed the carpet in the entrance, removing all traces of what had transpired the night before. But Clifford had no way of knowing that.

"There was one trail, however, that was uneven. It was deeper in some areas than others, as if whoever had been pushing the trolley was starting and stopping. None of the other trails looked that way, just one continuous push from the Client Area entrance to the door of the appropriate viewing room. That puzzled us a bit... at least until we found the shoe prints."

"You found shoe prints?"

This, too, was a lie. But McLean figured that two guys carrying a corpse would have been too visible, and one guy would struggle to move Sanford on his own. That meant a trolley was the logical solution. From there the other details started falling into place, helped by three pots of coffee and a refusal to sleep until McLean had a tale so complete even he almost believed it.

Someday he hoped to find out whether it was actually true.

"Well, perhaps toe prints would be a more accurate description. There wasn't a single flat print with heel like you'd get from the sole of a shoe anywhere within arm's distance of those unusual trolley marks."

"So what does that tell you?"

"That our bad guy was crawling. We're almost positive he pushed the trolley forward with his arms, then crawled on his hands and knees to catch up, then pushed again."

Watkins developed a sudden interest in the painting on the far wall.

"You might ask – we certainly did – why would a man do that? And do you know what the answer was?"

"I hope you're about to tell me."

"He wanted to stay low to the ground. Now why would anyone pushing a heavy load on a trolley want to stay low to the ground? It's much harder work that way. In fact, our crime scene analysts tried it, and were exhausted after about five minutes." McLean had to stifle a laugh; most of Scotland Yard's techies wouldn't have lasted 60 seconds in a crawling contest. "So why go to all that trouble? There's only one explanation we could come up with: the owner of the toe prints wanted to stay below the radar."

"I don't understand."

"Oh, I think you do, Mr. Watkins. In fact, you're one of very few people in the world who would understand. You knew the security systems at #42 Farringdon Road are designed to keep diamonds from getting out, not to keep dead bodies from getting in. You knew the cameras are focused on tables and countertops, which is where the diamonds are. You knew if you could stay below that level – by, say, crawling – and keep to the open spaces which the cameras don't cover, you could push the body of Mr. Sanford to the second floor coffee area and crawl back out without being seen."

"You certainly have an active imagination, Inspector. But if I knew all that about the security system, I'd also know there's simply no way for an outsider to get in the building in the first place."

"Unless you had inside help. A guard, say, who let you use his ID."

"Why would any guard who cares about keeping his job do that?"

"Money usually proves to be the answer. And I would have thought a billionaire such as yourself could make a very attractive offer, especially to someone who finds himself in urgent need of a few quid."

"So let me get this straight. You're saying a guard let me into the building, and gave me his ID so I could get past all the locked doors. But even though I had this carte blanche, I crawled along the ground to stay out of sight of the security cameras which otherwise would see I was pushing a trolley with a dead body on it. Is that about right?"

"A prosecutor couldn't have put it more concisely."

"And what proof, might I ask, have you got of what even you must admit is a rather far-fetched theory?"

"I think I'll save that until we meet in court."

"Should I be calling my lawyer, Inspector?"

"That choice is certainly available to you."

"What should I tell him the charge is, Inspector? Clearly not murder, since you told me the victim died of natural causes. Unlawful entry? If your theory is right, the guard let me in, so that wouldn't stick either. Crawling along the ground might be a bit odd, but as far as I know it's not illegal. Exactly what law do you plan to accuse me of breaking?"

"Desecration of a corpse, for starters. That gunshot to the chest of a dead man was totally unnecessary."

Johannesburg, March 23, 9:47 a.m.

"And you've got proof I was the one who fired the shot? Matched the ballistics with the gun I keep here in South Africa, perhaps?"

McLean had to admire the way Watkins kept throwing punches, despite knowing the fight was nearly over. "You know Mr. Sanford was shot somewhere other than #42 Farringdon Road."

"Which means you don't have the bullet. But suppose you did. How long's the sentence for desecration of a corpse, assuming it isn't just a fine?"

"Not very long. But it will keep you locked up long enough for us to sort out *why* you bothered with this elaborate ruse."

"Inspector, would I be right in thinking you just revealed the fact you don't have a motive for my supposed crime?"

"Oh, we have the motive all right. You were clearly being blackmailed over the sudden rise and equally fast fall of your diamond mine."

This was McLean's biggest bluff. He was pretty sure about the blackmail, but he didn't have a bit of proof. What's worse, he didn't have even an educated guess as to who was doing the blackmailing. Judging from where Clifford had dumped the body McLean's first thought had been Delacroix. But it just didn't make sense for a rich, powerful company to blackmail one fairly insignificant former employee. Or to put it more accurately, if Delacroix had wanted to crush Clifford Watkins, they had much easier ways to do it. But just because McLean couldn't explain the blackmail didn't mean he couldn't use it for leverage.

"Mr. Watkins, I'm a homicide detective. I have no authority over – and, to be honest, no interest in – financial crimes. I'll be sure to let my colleagues in London and Johannesburg know what I've found, and it's up to them what they do next. But if I were you, they would be the least of my worries."

"Why do you say that?"

"Because financial fraud is not a victimless crime. There's always somebody out there who's willing to do whatever it takes to – this is one of the few Americanisms I not only tolerate, but actually like – 'make himself whole'. If I were you, I'd rather hold hands with the law than the lawless."

Clifford tried to keep his face expressionless, but his mind kept looping footage of Frans with his 9mm Glock. "Inspector, you really have lost me. In fact, I wouldn't be surprised if your vivid imagination has left you behind as well. I am an honest businessman who has done nothing that would make me fear for my life."

"That's good to hear. You know, even homicide detectives don't like cleaning up after dead bodies."

CHAPTER 45

Gaborone, March 17, 11:45 a.m.

"What a bloody mess."

"What do you mean, boss?"

Lithwick threw the newspaper down in front of Frans, and pointed to the article. "Sanford's dead, and that idiot Watkins dumped his body inside Delacroix headquarters."

"Did Watkins kill him?"

"I seriously doubt it. He hasn't got the balls."

"Did the police arrest him?"

"The article doesn't even mention him. Maybe they don't know he was the one who dropped off the body."

"How do *you* know it was him?"

"Because I'm a goddamned psychic, Frans. The guy dies on the night he was meant to be picking up $32 million worth of diamonds from Watkins. His body is found at Delacroix, where Watkins used to work. And there was a note on the body saying REMEMBER GABORONE. Now do you think I might be on to something when I say it was Watkins?"

"Ok, boss, calm down. I wasn't trying to be insulting. Just trying to figure out what's going on." The big man then lowered his head, and slowly read the article.

"So where are the diamonds now?"

"I assume Watkins still has them."

"Want me to go get them?"

"What I want is for you to kill that bastard in a very slow and painful way." Frans immediately jumped to his feet. "Sit down, you fool. I didn't mean that literally. Just because the article doesn't mention Watkins doesn't mean the police don't know about him. He could be under surveillance. The last thing we want to do is walk right into the middle of a mess that up until now, at least, hasn't touched us."

"So we just give up on the money?"

"I don't know yet. I'll have to figure that out."

"At least you've still got your shares in All-African Diamonds."

"Which I'd better sell as fast as I can without attracting attention. Take away our big stones and that mine is just a worthless hole in the ground." Lithwick banged his fist on the table in frustration.

"So we're not going to use Watkins any more?" Frans asked."

"Not for now, at least. Until the dust settles Daniel Stern is a much safer bet."

"That's what we used to think about Watkins."

CHAPTER 46

London, March 25, 10:15 a.m.

"Thank you for agreeing to meet with me, Mr. Weil."

"Please call me Clarence. And thank *you*, Inspector, for offering to update me on this most troubling case."

"It is my pleasure, sir. If I may, let me explain what happened that night as we understand it. And then perhaps we could have a chat about what it all means."

"That would be excellent."

For the next 20 minutes, McLean laid out the story. He chose his words carefully, avoiding accusing Clifford Watkins of anything specific, but making damn sure that's the impression Weil took away from the conversation. While he spoke he watched the chairman carefully, especially during the part about the Future Vision Conference in Gaborone. He was hoping for some sort of reaction, a telltale twitch that would indicate what the man knew and what caught him by surprise. Perhaps it was Weil's habit of clasping his hands in front of his mouth, hiding everything below the nose. Or maybe it was the poker face, perfected over decades of negotiating multi-billion dollar deals. But McLean – an expert in body language – was getting absolutely nothing.

When he finished Weil said, "That's quite a story, Inspector. Can one assume all of it is not only true, but demonstrably so?"

McLean smiled; it was a masterly move. "I believe it to be true, sir, but you're right: there's very little proof for any of it."

"And is it your intention to find that proof?"

"Even if I wanted to, I couldn't. I'm a homicide detective, and while I do have a dead body I don't have a murder. So I will submit my report, and leave it to the Financial Crimes Unit to determine whether to proceed with other aspects of this case. But before I go, sir, would you mind if I gave you a few pieces of advice?"

This time Weil's eyes revealed surprise, but he quickly recovered and nodded his head in agreement.

"First, there's someone out there who knows – or thinks he knows – something he can use for blackmail. If he got away with it once, chances are he'll do it again. If at all possible, I'd find a way to clean up whatever he thinks he's got. Or at the very least, be prepared for it to go public.

Weil nodded in agreement, but his bobbing Adam's apple made it clear this was a sensitive area.

"Second, at least one person knows how to bypass your security system. He not only got in the building, he got out – without being seen. True, he didn't take any diamonds with him. But that seems easy in comparison to what's already been accomplished. Everything below desk level is currently your Achilles heel. I'd get that fixed as soon as possible."

This time the chairman's assent was both genuine and enthusiastic.

"Third, you have a crooked guard on your staff. I'll leave it to your security team to figure out who that is, and what to do about it. But in your shoes I would be checking into the private lives and finances of everyone on the security team on an ongoing basis. Just because they were clean and honest when you hired them doesn't mean they'll stay that way for their entire careers."

"That's very useful advice, thank you."

"Fourth, I am fairly certain the body was left on the second floor of this building in order to send a message *not* to the company itself, but to you personally. I think that's why it was a very public statement, but a very cryptic note."

"Why do you assume it was targeting me, rather than any of the 1,200 other people who work in this building?"

"You have the most to lose – both as chairman and as the majority shareholder – if the company is publicly humiliated. But even if I'm wrong, it's probably wise to think like someone who would do you harm, and do nothing and say nothing that would give him a stick to beat you with."

"Very well, Inspector. Is that it?"

"Just two more things, sir. My superiors are very concerned about word leaking out there was a security breach at #42 Farringdon Road. They think that will make it open season on this building, with everyone from sophisticated criminal gangs to drunken street thugs trying to get their hands on a few billion dollars worth of diamonds. You certainly don't need that threat, and neither, to be honest, does the Metropolitan Police. So today at noon there will be a press conference at which we announce that our investigation has revealed that John Sanford died of natural causes during a visit to Delacroix. That story has more holes than a sieve, but hopefully once murder is off the table the press will lose interest."

"That is very sensible, and very sensitive. Thank you for being so considerate."

"Which brings me to my final point, sir. My superiors would not be happy with what I'm about to say, and if you ever repeat a word of what I'm about to tell you I will deny it without hesitation."

"That's an unusual statement for an officer of the law."

"There is absolutely no doubt in my mind that Clifford Watkins is laundering blood diamonds by pretending to find them in the Orangevelt mine. I am equally certain he is doing it deliberately and with full knowledge. I have been unable to find out where he is getting those diamonds from – though I do have my suspicions. And some of those suspicions lead me back to this office."

"*What*?" Weil – who had sat calmly up to this moment – was outraged. "How can you sit there and accuse me of trading in blood diamonds?" he shouted. "Delacroix took the lead in setting up the Kimberley Process, and we've been its most vocal defender ever since. The only diamonds we touch are those that come from our own mines. If anything, we've gone too far in ensuring there's no possibility of diamonds from an area of conflict entering our supply chain, and that stance has cost us a significant amount of money." He was red-faced and winded when he finished.

"I'm aware of that, sir, and you are to be congratulated on your vision and your leadership. But it does seem strange Watkins had so little difficulty securing quite a large number of supposedly rare and exceptional diamonds."

"Maybe he bought them from someone who had been stockpiling the tainted goods until he found a buyer willing to overlook the Kimberley regulations."

"My thoughts precisely, sir. And that got me thinking about who might be in a position to do that. It would have to be someone with significant financial resources; someone who had contacts in places like Sierra Leone, Zimbabwe and the Congo; someone with the patience and vision to hold the goods – possibly for several years – until a buyer emerged."

"In this business there is no shortage of people with large amounts of cash, Inspector." Weil's defenses were now fully mounted; he would give up nothing.

"That's very true, sir. Though in most cases there'd be a paper trail linking the cash back to a bank loan. I think it's more likely the buyer was the head of a cash-rich private company."

"Like Delacroix. Is that what you're implying?"

"It's certainly one possibility. But what I found more intriguing than the financing was the lack of publicity."

"What do you mean?"

"I had my team do a little checking in the trade press. It seems every time a small mine finds a large stone, they immediately hold a press conference. It's good for building their brand, and good for driving up the share price."

"So?"

"So anyone who found the stones that were sold to Watkins would have made a fuss about them."

"Unless they were found in countries that weren't Kimberley compliant. No one would want to talk about *that* in public."

"Or if they were acquired *before* Kimberley, by a company with the financial wherewithal to keep them in the safe for years, and no need to publicly pat themselves on the back about the finds."

"And again you're implying that might be Delacroix." Weil was astonished by the man's willingness – eagerness – to make legally actionable allegations with no substantiation whatsoever. And he was treating Weil's company, once the victim of a crime, like a criminal. Weil found McLean's lack of professional integrity shocking.

"There's no question the description fits. But that means nothing without proof that Delacroix not only *could* have helped Watkins get the diamonds, but actually did."

"And is it your intention to go in search of that proof?"

"As I said, Mr. Chairman, I'm in homicide, not financial crimes. And people above my pay grade have decided that the less that is publicly known about this incident, the better. So this story ends here and now. My objective in telling you all this is to emphasize one would be wise not to write another chapter."

Weil stood, and offered his hand. "I think we can both agree on that."

THE END

ACKNOWLEDGEMENTS

This book began several years ago, at a time when I was spending much of my life on airplanes and the rest wondering why modern science had failed to find a cure for jet lag. Night after sleepless night I reworked the story in my head, so when I was finally able to put fingers to keyboard the words flowed like water from a just-opened dam. In no time at all I had a book that was both brilliantly plotted and beautifully written.

It was also 11 pages long.

Thus began the painful process of learning to write a novel. Fortunately my old friend Ed Sikov is a highly successful author, a remarkably patient editor, and an indefatigably enthusiastic cheerleader for the wannabe writer in me. It is no exaggeration to say this book would not exist without him.

I'm also indebted to Larissa Makhotkina, my toughest critic and one with the tremendously annoying habit of almost always being right.

Thanks go to Davy Lapa, one of the world's great diamantaires, for ensuring the technical information is within spitting distance of correct. Invaluable help also came from Ricky Ng, who calculated the price of diamonds far larger than I'm ever likely to see.

Warm kisses to Thoko Modisakeng for teaching me how to speak tough guy in Afrikaans, and happily agreeing to lend her name to a Gaborone prostitute.

The concept for the cover visual is from the brilliant mind of David Kan.

Thank you to the good people at De Beers for letting me spend a decade in the incredible world of diamonds. I'm also indebted to the many, many people within the industry who shared their knowledge, their stories and their friendship; I truly hope you enjoyed this book.

The longest of hugs to my darling daughter Julia, whose surprisingly good proofreading skills convinced me the investment in her college education was money well spent.

A deep bow and a domo arigato gozaimashita to my saintly wife Kaoru, who had me underfoot for an entire year and didn't complain once.

But most of all, thank *you* for buying (hopefully!) this book and for reading to the very last...word.

David W. Rudlin
March 28, 2013
Tokyo, Japan

Made in the USA
Charleston, SC
24 August 2013